JENNA'S JOURNEY

BOOK 1 - HEARTSGATE HEALING

KAY P. DAWSON

CHAPTER 1

"Jenna, I know you're sick of me saying this, but I just don't think you've thought this through. I know what we've seen happen, and there's no doubt these people are going *somewhere*. But, I still don't know how much I trust that purple-haired crazy woman. What if you get sent back in time to somewhere awful and you can't stand it? Then what will happen? You're prepared to just die alone, who knows where, without anyone you know around you?"

Jenna closed her eyes for a second, rolling them without her friend being able to see. Carly was always a little more dramatic than was required in a situation, and she'd known out of her two best friends, Carly would be the one with the biggest arguments about her going.

"I'm not going to just go off and die alone, Carly. Dr. Lachele has been honest about everything that happens when she lets us make our wishes. She's also assured us that the other book club members who have gone before me are completely happy with the lives they're now living. And that's what I want for myself."

"But, Jenna, the difference is that those people were all going toward something they wanted. You're running away from something. That's a big difference."

Jenna smiled at her less dramatic friend, Devyn. "That's true, but I've spoken with Dr. Lachele a lot over the past couple of weeks, and she's assured me that there is always the chance for a better life if we're willing to take that risk, no matter what the reasons." She zipped up her smaller bag she'd been packing and set it on top of the antique trunk she'd bought on a whim over three years ago. It had been meant to only be used as an interesting piece of decor in her apartment but would now carry the few possessions she could take with her when she let Dr. Lachele send her back in time.

"Did they even use zippers back then?" Carly asked, pointing to her bag, eyebrows raised in a way that suggested Jenna really didn't know what she was doing.

"I don't even know." She sighed, emptying everything into a canvas bag instead, just in case. "But look, not only is there a chance of a better life, but there's a chance for love. Real love. With someone who won't cheat on me multiple times, then stalk me, and make me scared for my own life when I've finally had enough and leave him."

She looked out the window at the people walking on the streets below. When she'd moved to Heartsgate after finishing high school, the town had held such promise for her after growing up in New York City. The name alone had inspired her to believe things would be better.

Of course, anything would have been better than being shuffled from home to home in the foster system that had let her, and her friends, down for so many years. She'd never had a real home, or a family, other than the two girls standing in this tiny apartment with her right now.

Carly came over and put her hand on her shoulder, looking out the window with her. "It's not fair that David gets to win like this."

Jenna turned to face her, shaking her head. "He's not winning, Carly. Don't you see? I have a chance to get away from him, while starting a brand-new life. This is the adventure I've always dreamed about." She glanced over at Devyn and smiled. "We've all dreamed of doing something daring and fun. How many times have we 'lived' the stories we were reading about? And talked about how wonderful it would be to have lived in a different time, when things were simpler, and the men treated their women like queens?"

"Well, *talking* about it and actually *doing* it are two different things. Do you honestly believe things were simpler back in the pioneer days? Especially on the Oregon Trail? And I doubt the men were really any better back then than they are now."

Jenna grinned widely, knowing in her heart she was doing the right thing. Even if she couldn't convince her friends, she knew today she was going on the adventure she'd always dreamed about.

"It's something we always said we'd like to do. We've planned out our entire trip, including taking the covered wagon on overnight stops to various places along the way while seeing all of the historical sites." She shrugged and laughed quietly. "Think how much better it will be to do it in real time."

Across the room, her phone vibrated against the wooden table where it rested. They all looked at it, knowing it was him calling again. He wouldn't give up. He never did.

"I know it's crazy, guys. But I'm scared. I'm scared if I stay here, this will be my life forever. Always on edge and waiting for the day he finally follows through on his threats. I can't get away from him here." She swallowed hard, trying not to let the tears fall. "You know I'm going to miss you both. You've been my friends for as long back as I can remember, and I know I would have never survived all those years without you. I'm going to miss you both fiercely."

The tears she'd been holding back rolled down her cheeks, as her friends both came and wrapped their arms around her.

"Jenna, we'll miss you too. But I know you'll be okay. And I hope you find someone who loves you the way you deserve." Carly wiped at her eyes as she pulled back and looked at her. "At least you're going and trying, instead of sitting around and waiting for Luke Bryan to notice her like someone else we know."

They all laughed, trying to lift their spirits in the moment, as Carly tilted her head toward Devyn, who stuck her tongue out back at her. "I never said it has to *be* Luke Bryan…just someone exactly like him. That's not really too much to ask."

It had been a running joke with the girls for years, with Devyn having a mad crush on the famous country singer. She'd always said there was no one else who would ever be able to have her heart like Luke Bryan.

"All right. Let's get this stuff over to the book club meeting so Dr. Lachele can work her magic." Devyn turned and clapped her hands, but Jenna saw the tears she was trying to hide.

Even though she had thought this over every minute of the day for the past few weeks, Jenna still had a twinge of doubt. She just hoped when she got to the meeting, where Dr. Lachele was waiting to grant her the wish of going back in time, she wouldn't chicken out.

Because she knew if she stayed here, her life could never go back to what it was before she met her ex.

This was her only option for a safe and happy future. And finding someone to love.

"OH MY GOODNESS, you brought an entire trunk with you!"

Dr. Lachele breezed over in a flurry of skirts, her purple hair reflecting from the sunlight peeking in the window of the room where the book club met in the library every week.

"Well, you told me to make sure I had what I needed. And I figured, since I'm going on the Oregon Trail, a trunk wouldn't look entirely out of place when I just show up there."

"You're right about that. And I see you've dressed for the time period too." Dr. Lachele grinned as she reached out to touch the fabric of the skirt Carly had sewn for her. "This looks just perfect. Well suited for days on the trail." She shook her head and laughed as she flipped a hand in the air. "I still can't understand why you'd choose such a place of hardship for your place to go, but who am I to judge? The heart leads where it needs to go."

Jenna laughed nervously as she looked around at all the other book club members. In the past few weeks, ever since the day Dr. Lachele had turned up at their meetings, everyone had grown quite well acquainted as they watched the magic the purple-haired woman performed.

She remembered the first time they'd watched as Heather was "poofed" away to the Highlands. In shock, they'd been unsure at what they'd witnessed. Then when the man who'd shown up by accident one day magically disappeared after making a wish, the rest of them hadn't been able to deny what they were seeing.

It still seemed so unbelievable, but after Dr. Lachele had assured them that the people who'd been granted their wishes were all right, and in truth, were following on their heart's path, it had been easier to believe.

And, it was what was leading her own heart today.

"What all did you pack in here? You know you need to be careful with whatever you take that it isn't used in any way that can change history."

"I know. Carly made me a couple of extra skirts and dresses to wear because I need to have a regular change of clothes. I've also included my own under-garments, some feminine supplies that I'm not prepared to live without, especially while on the trail, a few bottles of my favorite shampoo and body wash, and of course, sunscreen. I've also packed an extra pair of boots that look like they could fit in the time period, and have put cushion insoles in all of my shoes to make sure the walk is easier on my feet."

Dr. Lachele laughed and clapped her hands together. "Oh, you're so practical compared to some of the people I've sent back."

Jenna's cheeks heated up and she smiled sheepishly at Dr. Lachele. "Well, I did also pack my e-reader and a solar charger. I've loaded it up with enough books to last me at least a year, I hope. That's the one thing I would miss more than anything."

"Of course, you would. We can live without television or our phones, but if we had no books, I'm quite sure we'd all go mad."

"And, you can restock some of my supplies as needed, until I can maybe learn to adjust and live without them, right? Although I don't think I can ever live without sunscreen. Or my shampoos. Well, any of it really."

Nervousness was starting to creep in, and she knew she'd have to get Dr. Lachele to perform her magic before she changed her mind.

The kind, older woman must have sensed her worries, because she reached out to touch her arm and smiled. "My dear, I will always be available to you if you need me. And I will keep you stocked in anything you need. I'm not going to just whisk you off to some scary place and leave you forever. I will come and check in on you to make sure you've found your destiny."

"How can you be sure this is my destiny?" Jenna still didn't know if it could be true. "I don't know if I can trust myself to find someone to love, who won't end up treating me the way others have in the past. I'm just looking for peace and happiness."

Dr. Lachele just smiled as she leaned in closer to speak only to her. "That's quite all right. Because one thing I've learned about magic, is that it doesn't matter if you're looking for love. Sometimes, it just finds you where you least expect it. It might even fall right on top of you. Now, are you ready to follow the path that's always been ready for you?"

Jenna nodded, taking one last look at her friends standing to the side. They'd said their goodbyes already, and the reassuring smiles on their faces told her she was doing the right thing.

"You know what to do." Dr. Lachele stepped back and waited.

"I wish I could go back in time, to journey along the Oregon Trail, and find my chance at happiness."

And with those words, the world around her

started to spin. Her last thought before everything went dark was that even if she never did find love again, at least now she was finally free from her ex.

Her new life was just beginning.

*a*dam pulled hard on the leather strap, making sure it was secure before they started off on the trail. He'd been up since before the sun, and he was already tired from trying to get everyone organized and ready. He cringed as he pulled the next strap, thinking about the day he'd decided he was heading west.

It had seemed so simple. It was going to be just him. A chance to go west and see some of the world —do what his uncle Mike had wanted to do his whole life, but never had the opportunity before he died.

But then his mother, who he loved dearly and could never say no to, decided she was going as well. Since Adam was planning to go out to Oregon and work with family, she'd wanted to come and stay with her sister-in-law she hadn't seen in years. And since his mother was a widow, she had nothing holding her back here if her only son was leaving.

Then, as if that wasn't enough, Charlotte—the woman who'd decided she was going to marry him —had let him know a week ago that she'd be joining him in the move out to Oregon. Her brother Nelson would be accompanying them because he had plans to open a new business out west, believing there was unlimited money to be made.

At one point, when he was younger, he'd been interested in her, but she'd never returned any of his attention, so he'd stopped making a fool of himself. Despite that, Adam had never given Charlotte any reason to believe they'd be married, other than the fact he'd known her his whole life, and everyone had just always assumed it would happen. They were the closest to age in the small community he'd come from, and there weren't a whole lot of women to choose from. Perhaps it would have happened at some point, but it wasn't something he had on his mind right now.

His uncle Mike had shown him how much fun could be had as a bachelor, and Adam just wasn't ready to give his own bachelorhood up just yet. He'd tried to tell Charlotte that, and that he'd come back and take her out there when he was ready.

He groaned to himself, frustrated that a trip he could have made on his own at a much faster pace was now requiring him to join a wagon train headed west, which would take months to arrive at their destination.

Things couldn't get any worse if he tried.

Backing up, his foot tangled in something on the ground, leaving him off-balance and flailing to keep from falling. As he lost the battle, he quickly realized it was a woman lying on the ground and he was about to land square on top of her.

Throwing himself to the side at the last minute, he hit the ground in a cloud of dust and had the air knocked out of his lungs. He lay their stunned for a few seconds, trying to catch his breath.

"What are you doing on the ground behind my wagon? Where did you even come from?" His voice was raw as he struggled to breathe. He knew there hadn't been a woman lying on the ground a minute ago. He might not always be the most observant man, but he was quite certain he would have noticed that.

"Oh, my goodness. I'm so sorry. I thought I would have landed somewhere a little less in the way." Her hand shot up to cover her mouth. "I mean, I must have fallen asleep here and you didn't see me until now."

His eyebrows pulled together as he tried to make sense of what was going on. His backside hurt from landing on the hard, baked ground, and he already wasn't in a good mood with needing to outfit an entire wagon filled with his mother's belongings.

"Ma'am, I assure you, I'd have noticed a woman sprawled on the ground beside a trunk the size of my wagon."

She quickly turned to look at her trunk. "Is it too big? Isn't this what you would use for a trip on a wagon train?"

He jumped to his feet, then put his hand out to help her as she struggled to stand up, catching her skirt under her foot as she did. She stumbled forward, bumping into him without ever taking his offered hand.

He steadied her, holding her shoulders as she mumbled under her breath, "These skirts are going to be the death of me."

"I beg your pardon, ma'am?"

She stopped fussing and looked at him, then stepped back and brought her hand up to right the bonnet that had become twisted on her head. When her eyes met his, the breath he'd finally managed to catch, was ripped from his lungs again.

He was sure in all his life he'd never seen a woman with eyes bluer than the sky above them, made even brighter by the whiteness of the skin framing them.

"I'm sorry. I'm just feeling hopelessly lost right now. If I could just have a moment to let my brain catch up to everything..."

His eyebrows were now stuck in a frown as he listened to her speak. He'd never heard anyone, never mind a woman, talk the way she did. He wasn't sure if it was the accent, or just the words she was using. But something didn't seem right to him.

"Who are you here with?"

He watched her closely, while her gaze roamed around, looking at the many wagons getting ready to head out in less than an hour. Her dark red hair poked out around the sides of the bonnet as she fiddled with the straps, her eyes darting back and forth as people rushed around them.

"Well, um...I'm not really sure."

If he hadn't been starting to wonder about her sanity, he was beginning to question it now. She might be beautiful, but it was quite obvious her mind was addled.

"Adam, are you finished?"

He turned to look at his mother who was coming around to the back of the wagon. Her face lit up in a smile as soon as she noticed the woman standing beside him. "Well, hello! It's nice to meet some of the other women who I'll be sharing time with over the next few weeks along the trail." As she came over, she tapped him on the arm. "Adam, remember your manners. Can you introduce me to the young lady you've been talking with?"

He chuckled and raised an eyebrow as he shrugged. "I'm afraid I haven't had the good fortune to get her name yet, Mother. I had just quite literally stumbled over her before you came along."

"Oh, I apologize for my son's lack of manners. My name is Mrs. Mary Wallace. My friends and family call me Minnie."

The other woman smiled warmly at his mother, and he noted her dimples. "My name is Jenna Hart."

"It's very nice to meet you, Miss Hart. This is my son, Adam Wallace."

He nodded at the woman, suddenly irritated by the whole situation. He didn't have time to be standing around making small talk and introductions to strange women who were sleeping on the ground.

"If you'll excuse me, Miss Hart. I've got a wagon to get ready."

He ignored the stern look his mother sent in his direction as he walked away. Truthfully, he'd done everything he needed to do and had double checked everything in preparation for the day ahead.

But something about those bright blue eyes looking at him had been unnerving. He couldn't explain it, but he had sense that he needed to protect her from something, and he couldn't figure out why or what. And the last thing he needed was one more person to look after.

As the wagons prepared to head out, he was asked to check over a few of the wheels and harnesses being hooked up. A blacksmith by trade, he'd been assigned the job of providing services over the weeks ahead to his fellow travelers if needed.

By the time he got back to the wagon, he was more than ready for things to get moving.

Charlotte was standing beside the wagon, laughing at something her brother was telling her. Adam looked at his wagon, then over to the one they were using. "How come none of the oxen have been hooked up?"

Nelson scoffed and laughed. "Adam, you've known me for years. I'm a businessman. When do you suppose I would have ever worked with animals this large?"

Adam's mouth dropped as he looked at the man in disbelief. "So, you think I'll be taking care of your team the whole way?"

"Well, I'll do my best to help as I can. I would think you'd be thankful for me closing my store so I could accompany my sister out west for you. But I'm not going to be much help with the livestock, I'm afraid."

Taking a deep breath, Adam bit his tongue as he walked over to start hooking the teams up. He knew he should be grateful to Nelson for bringing Charlotte, and most men would be thrilled about it. Charlotte was a stunning woman, and he did like her a great deal. He knew that some day, she would make a fine wife. In fact, when he was younger, he'd been the one to do the pursuing while she'd seemed less interested in his intentions.

So, the fact that she was suddenly so excited to follow him out to Oregon, planning to spend her life with him, still confused him.

His head pounded as he got the yoke put over the animals, which were now hooked to Nelson and Charlotte's wagon. He reached up to wipe the sweat from his forehead, catching his breath before he went to get his own team ready.

As he stepped back, the back of his legs bumped into something hard, sending him falling backward for the second time already today. He landed on his back, with his legs still hung over the top of a trunk he recognized from earlier.

He clenched his eyes shut and counted to five in his head before opening them to look up into the faces of his mother and Miss Hart.

The blue eyes peeking out from beneath the bonnet were wide, and her hand had come up to cover her mouth. If he didn't know how impolite it would be, and completely improper for a lady, he was almost certain she was struggling not to laugh at him.

"For goodness sakes, Adam. Didn't you hear us come up behind you and set the trunk down? You were so busy muttering under your breath, I guess you didn't notice."

He pulled his legs off the trunk and stood up, wiping the dust off his clothes. They hadn't even gotten on the trail yet and his clothes were covered in dirt from being on the ground so many times.

"No, Mother. I was a bit busy. Can I ask why this trunk is sitting here?"

Something in the way she looked over and smiled widely at the other woman filled him with dread. He knew what she was going to say before she'd even said the words.

"Well, Miss Hart, has found herself without a wagon to take her west, so I've invited her to join us."

CHAPTER 3

Jenna peered over at the man who had literally fallen on top of her when she'd wished herself here. She knew he wasn't happy about her joining them and she couldn't really blame him. It appeared as though he already had quite a few people to be responsible for over the weeks ahead, so one more person wasn't something he'd been looking for.

He'd tried to be polite, leading his mother away to discuss things out of Jenna's earshot. But she'd heard them talking and now she wished maybe she'd thought things through a little bit better before letting Dr. Lachele work her magic.

Being whisked into another time without a real plan wasn't a good idea. These pioneers were already packed to go, with all their belongings and supplies. She shouldn't have just expected someone would have room to let her tag along.

Adam hadn't been happy about having another mouth to feed, having to ration the food they'd packed. Not to mention one more trunk to try cramming into the already full wagon, laden with food supplies, water barrels, and spare wagon parts. It was much smaller than she'd expected.

Now, they were on the move, and she was walking alongside the wagons that would take her west. She hoped her boots held up; it was going to be a long walk…

"So, you never really mentioned where you came from. Your accent is quite different from anything I've heard before."

Jenna smiled at the younger woman walking beside her. Mrs. Wallace had introduced her to Charlotte and Nelson Kent before they'd left, letting her know they would all be traveling together. While Mrs. Wallace hadn't said Charlotte was Adam's fiancée, it was obvious the younger woman considered herself to be.

"I grew up in New York City."

"Funny, I've met so many people from New York and your accent is just so unique."

Jenna got the impression the woman wasn't happy about her being with them. She wished she could just tell her not to worry because the last thing Jenna wanted to do was steal her man. While he was quite astonishingly good-looking and exactly how she'd always pictured the rough, frontier cowboy to be, he wasn't really her type.

Besides, she was pretty sure Dr. Lachele wouldn't have dropped her in the lap of a man who was engaged to be married. She knew there was someone on this wagon train she was meant to fall in love with, but she wasn't ready to start looking for who that might be yet.

"And why are you heading west? Especially all alone. Don't you think it's a bit dangerous?"

Jenna looked down and wiped at her skirt, making sure it was still covering her boots. She worried they weren't similar enough to what they wore and didn't want to draw attention to them. "Well, I know it's quite dangerous. But I just needed a new beginning somewhere far away from home. So, I figured this would be my best bet."

Charlotte looked at her sideways as she listened, reminding Jenna she needed to be careful how she spoke. The manner of speaking back in this time was quite different than she was used to, so she was going to have to keep reminding herself to fit in better.

"What are you planning to do when you get out there?"

"Now, Charlotte, let's give Miss Hart some time to get settled in before we ask her all the questions. She was in need of an escort to take her west, and I was raised to help others out when you can. So, what she's planning to do when she gets west, and her reasons for going, are her own concern."

Jenna smiled thankfully at Mrs. Wallace who was walking on the other side of her. They'd only set out an hour ago and already Jenna was hot and thirsty, so the last thing she wanted to deal with right now was a hundred questions from a jealous girlfriend.

The older woman had been exactly who she needed when she'd ended up here. After Adam had left them alone behind the wagon, Mrs. Wallace had been so kind, offering her the chance to explain why she was alone, and trying to join a wagon train headed west.

Of course, Jenna hadn't really known how to explain it, so she'd told the truth and said she was hoping for the chance at a new life. But then, out of nowhere, Jenna had been hit with the stress of everything from the past few months and leaving everything she knew behind. Tears had suddenly streamed down her cheeks, and no matter how hard she'd tried to act like she was fine, Mrs. Wallace had come over and wrapped her in a gentle embrace to soothe her.

In all her life, Jenna had never had a mother figure care enough to do something like that, and it had caught her off guard. After pulling herself together, she'd stepped back and tried to act like she was stronger than she was feeling.

Mrs. Wallace had simply told her she would be joining them on the journey west, and she wasn't taking no for an answer.

"Thank you again, Mrs. Wallace, for letting me come with you. I know it won't be easy adding another mouth to feed from your supplies. When we get to the closest fort, I will try to get some more provisions for myself to add to what you have. And I promise I'll do my part to pitch in however I can, to make things a little easier. Although I admit, I'm a bit worried about cooking on the trail. It's going to be a lot to learn."

If they only knew just how much she was going to have to learn. Jenna hadn't even been much of a cook with all the modern appliances and fresh food back home, so this was going to be a big challenge to prove herself out here.

"Please, I've asked you to call me Minnie. That's what friends and family call me, and we are going to be spending a great deal of time together these next few months."

Jenna pulled at her bonnet, making sure it was covering her face. She missed her worn old baseball cap that she could poke her ponytail through, but truthfully, this bonnet was much more practical for the days ahead. She'd been too afraid to hold anyone up by trying to sneak into her trunk to get her sunscreen out, so she hadn't put any on today. With her skin, if the sun even peeked in under her bonnet, it was going to be on fire by nightfall.

"Okay, Minnie. And you can both call me Jenna."

Since she'd arrived, everyone had called her Miss Hart, and it was something Jenna didn't think she would ever get used to. She understood how formalities were back in this time, but it still felt strange to be addressed this way. And the more people she could call by first name, the easier it would be for her to remember.

"My poor feet are already killing me. I'm going to go ride in your wagon, Minnie, so I can talk a bit with Adam. He looked quite burdened this morning, so perhaps having me closer will be good for him."

Jenna watched Charlotte race ahead to the wagon Adam was driving. The oxen had rings through their noses, and ropes were tied to lead them along the trail. He was walking ahead of them, guiding them over the rough ground. Jenna knew from everything she'd read about the Oregon Trail over the years that she would also be walking most of the way, which was equally terrifying and exciting. The wagons were not comfortable to ride in over the bumpy trail, and the one she'd put her trunk in didn't have much space to spare anyway.

But Charlotte had asked Adam to stop the wagon and was letting him assist her up into the front seat. He didn't seem too happy about having to stop and quickly went back to the front of the animals to keep moving when she was sitting down.

"I hope your son isn't too upset with having me tag along. He seems quite annoyed with everything since I met him, and I guess I can't really blame him. I know he probably thinks he's going to be responsible for me too now, not to mention he tripped over top of me and my trunk twice within moments of meeting me. It's not exactly the nice introduction a person could hope for."

"Oh, don't worry about him. He's had a bee in his britches ever since I let him know I was going west too. Then, of course, Charlotte and her brother decided to come as well, and he wasn't too happy about that either. He'd planned on hopping on his horse and heading west on his own, so having to do it this way has left him a little more grumpy than he usually is." Minnie laughed and hooked her arm through hers as they walked along the side of the wagon. "I'm so glad to have you for company on this journey. I fear I'd have gone quite mad if I'd had to listen to his grumbling every day."

Jenna laughed loudly, causing Adam to turn and look at her. She clamped her hand over her mouth, reminding herself she needed to rein in her "cackling laugh" as her friends had always called it.

"Well, you would have had Charlotte for company."

Minnie just clucked her tongue and rolled her eyes. "Charlotte is a nice enough girl, and I'd never say anything bad about anyone, but she's not someone I would consider good company on a trip like this. She won't be able to stand the grueling days of walking. Besides, she's going to spend all her time trying to get Adam to propose to her, so I doubt she'll want to walk alongside me anyway."

Jenna watched the woman who was now sitting in the front of the wagon, desperately trying to hang onto the side of the seat as it bounced over the ruts. It was clear she wasn't comfortable but if her feet were already sore, Jenna figured it was probably the best place for her.

Adam wasn't paying her any attention as he led the animals over the first leg of the trail. They'd been told they wouldn't go too far today so they could give the animals and people the chance to ease into the routine of travel. He was making sure all the livestock they'd brought would be ready for the days ahead, so he was more focused on the oxen beside him than the woman in the wagon.

"I must have misunderstood, but I thought Charlotte was already his fiancée. How come he wasn't excited for her to come with him?"

"Oh, they're not engaged. Charlotte just believes they will be. She never had any interest in him until recently, no matter how much attention he gave her. By the time he decided to head out west, he'd given up on trying for her affections. Then all of a sudden, she wanted to come too." Minnie shook her head. "I've never really trusted her, but if she's the one my son decides to marry, I will accept it."

Jenna's eyes were drawn to the other man in their

company who was leading the wagon ahead of Adam. She had to bite her lip to stop herself from laughing when she noticed Charlotte's brother struggling to stay far enough away from his team of oxen, so they wouldn't crush him. He was dressed in a suit that Jenna knew had to be too warm for the day. It was still spring, but there was a lot of heat in the sun beating down on them.

And, instead of the wide-brimmed hat Adam and most of the other men were wearing, Nelson had a fancy top hat on his head. It just seemed so out of place here on the trail, and especially on someone leading a team of oxen over bumpy, rough ground.

But she had noticed that he was quite good-looking underneath all of his "finery." She'd always been drawn to men with blond hair, and when he'd taken his hat off during their introduction, she'd been surprised at how neatly cut it was.

He was the complete opposite of the first man she'd met when she arrived. Adam had dark hair that hung in waves beneath his rough-looking hat. He was nothing like the men she'd ever been attracted to.

Which had her feeling quite confused when she remembered talking to Dr. Lachele about her wish a few weeks ago. When Jenna had asked her how she would possibly know who her soul mate was when she got there, Dr. Lachele had smiled and told her she would have no doubt. He would be one of the first people she would meet.

But Adam was heading west with a woman who he was probably going to marry. And he wasn't at all the kind of guy she ever dated. She preferred men who smiled once in a while.

Jenna wondered if this time, maybe, Dr. Lachele had gotten a bit mixed up. Was Nelson the one she was really supposed to find? She'd met him soon after arriving.

When she looked back and forth between the two of them, she knew who the logical choice would be. And Nelson seemed nice, compared to the man she'd left behind.

Her stomach did a little somersault when she realized she was actually in the company of the man who was supposed to give her the love she'd been searching for.

He had to be the one she'd been sent here for.

So why then did her gaze keep moving to the scowling man with the overly long hair, who was leading a wagon where his future bride was riding?

CHAPTER 4

*A*dam leaned back against the wheel of the wagon, watching the woman who was trying to help his mother prepare a meal. Charlotte had gone to have a rest in the back of her wagon after their first few hours on the trail, claiming to have an aching head, leaving just the two women to do the cooking.

Everything had gone fairly smoothly for their first day after leaving Independence, but he was glad they'd stopped early. The worry of making sure everything was organized was catching up to him and he was exhausted. They'd already traveled from St. Louis to the kicking off point, so everyone was more than a bit tired. They'd rested a few days while stocking up on supplies for the journey ahead and getting on with the wagon train that was preparing to leave, but it hadn't been long enough.

He knew he'd been a bit more ornery than usual when they'd set off this morning. But ever since he'd fallen over top of the woman who was now hunched over peeling potatoes beside his mother, he hadn't been able to control his mood.

As he watched, she lifted her head and wiped at her brow with the back of her arm. Her red hair was poking out everywhere under her bonnet, and he had to smile as she blew a curl away from her eyes, only to have it fall back down. He knew it had been a hard day for her, but she hadn't complained about anything.

His mother seemed quite happy to have her along as company, so he figured maybe it wasn't all bad to have one more person to look after. He still had serious doubts that Charlotte would make it past the first fort before wanting to go home, so at least his mother would still have a female companion for the rest of the way.

He stood up, stretching his back and cringed at the loud cracking he heard. If he was in this kind of shape after just one day, how would he be by the end of the trip?

He reminded himself he had fallen quite hard on

his backside more than once today, so he was sure that contributed to his aching bones.

"Adam, could you help Jenna with these potatoes? I need to get the pork put on the fire."

He raised his eyebrow and laughed. "Mother, have you ever seen me peel a potato?"

"I don't care if you have or not. You're doing it today. We'll all have to learn to do things we haven't done before if we're going to make it to Oregon in one piece."

He went over and sat on the crate his mother had just vacated, taking the knife she thrust into his hands. He glanced over at the woman beside him and laughed when he saw the look of concentration on her face. She had her eyes pulled together, causing crinkles around the bridge of her nose. The potato she was holding had been peeled so far back there was barely anything left.

"You know we only have enough potatoes for the first few days of the trail, so we should try to make them last. If you keep peeling them to the size of a pea, I'm afraid we'll be out before tomorrow."

She lifted her head and relaxed her eyes. She looked at the small piece of potato held in her hand and chuckled. "You're right. I was so focused on getting all the peel off, I didn't even realize what I was doing. I've never really been the one who did the cooking before, so I'm afraid it's going to take me some time to learn how to do it properly out here."

He wondered why a woman her age wouldn't know how to cook. "Did you have servants who did your cooking for you?"

She looked at him in confusion for a few seconds, then let out a loud laugh. It was a sound he'd never heard from a lady before, but something about it made him laugh too, not even knowing why.

"No, I didn't have any servants. I had a lot of take out or else went to my friend Carly's place. She loved to cook so I was more than happy to let her experiment with her latest recipe."

He stared at her in confusion. "What is take out exactly?"

Her mouth opened in an "o" shape and her eyes widened as she stared back at him. "Um, well, I mean...I wasn't really serious. I did do a lot of cooking, as women are expected to do in this time, but I'm just not really good at it. And being out here is quite different, so I'm going to have to learn new ways to cook."

Adam wasn't sure what she was hiding, but he

knew something just didn't seem right. "Where did you say you were from again?"

She grabbed another potato and began jamming the knife into it. "New York."

"Is your family still there? Why are you heading out west on your own?"

She continued working, not meeting his eyes. "I don't have any family. So no one's going to miss me. I had the chance to go away and start a new life, so I decided to do it. I've always wanted the adventure and figured now was as good a time as any."

He felt bad asking about her family, sensing that it had upset her. He couldn't believe there wasn't anyone out there who would miss her, but he didn't want to keep pushing her. They were going to have more than enough time over the weeks ahead for him to find out more about her.

What he didn't understand was why he was so curious about her in the first place.

JENNA DUG into her trunk to find another shawl. One thing she did know how to do was knit, so she'd made a couple of warm sweaters and shawls to bring, knowing there would be many nights that would be chilly.

She saw her sunscreen, and pulled it to the top to make it easier to get to in the morning. Seeing her shampoo bottle, she closed her eyes and sighed, wishing fervently that she could somehow have a shower. She'd known this was going to be hard, but until she'd spent the first day walking in the dust of the trail and sweating everywhere, she hadn't realized how much.

She'd gone to the river they were camped near earlier to wash off the top layer of dust, but she'd always been the girl who showered at least once a day, if not more.

This was going to be an adjustment, but thankfully, she'd brought her deodorant. And she would figure out how to wash thoroughly with a cloth and her shampoo once she was feeling a bit more settled.

Her body ached everywhere from walking, and then having to work so hard at getting supper prepared and cooked, setting the small tent up she would be sharing with Minnie, and then cleaning up from the meal. She knew everyone had thought her strange when she'd brought water from the river and boiled it on a pot over the fire, letting it cool before drinking it.

One thing Dr. Lachele had said was not to try changing history, but Jenna didn't think explaining to her fellow travelers that boiling water made it safer to drink was altering things too much. She'd read about some women on the Oregon Trail boiling water to get rid of bugs and floaty things, so she figured there was already some knowledge about it back then anyway. Or now. She wasn't quite sure how to think about the time she was in.

But one thing she wasn't prepared to compromise on was her drinking water. Jenna knew the risks of contaminated water, and if it could keep her and her companions safer, she would take the time to boil water every day if she could and put some in the wagon's barrels.

Even if they did think she was strange for doing so.

"Jenna? It's time to milk Annie. You said you'd like to help, so I can teach you if you'd like."

She jumped as Minnie called into the back of the wagon, quickly closing the lid on her trunk.

"Of course. I feel rather silly that I've never milked a cow before, so I appreciate you taking the time to show me. I want to pull my weight."

She cringed as she climbed out of the wagon, wondering if that was a term they would have used in this time period. One thing she was having trouble with was using the proper manner of speech.

But Minnie hadn't seemed to notice as they walked over to where the milk cow, Annie, was tied to the side of the wagon.

"Charlotte still has a bit of a headache, so I guess it will just be us. The poor girl, I'm not sure how she's going to make it all the way to Oregon."

Jenna could tell Minnie was annoyed. As they'd eaten their meal, she'd told the girls they would all take turns with milking. They would milk every evening before bed, then strain it into small buckets, cover and leave them under the wagon until morning. There would be a nice thick cream they could then put in the churn that was tied down in the back of the wagon, along with the last bit of milk from the morning milking. As the wagon bounced along during the day, it would form into butter for their evening meal.

Jenna had to smile. To be honest, she'd never really thought about how butter was made. It just came in a paper wrap that you bought at the grocery store in the dairy section. And now she'd be *making* it herself. This was fun.

Jenna could see how important this task was going to be. Not only would they have milk and cream, but it would provide them with the butter over the days ahead.

"I guess I'll have to show Charlotte another day. Her father owned the mercantile in town so milking cows wasn't something she ever learned."

"I grew up in the city and never had the chance to learn either. I hope I don't do anything to hurt her." Jenna edged closer to the large cow—the mobile dairy section and organic to boot—that was standing grazing and not even paying any attention to them.

Minnie laughed and set the small stool she was carrying next to the cow.

"Annie is a tough old girl. And she's as sweet as sugar, so you don't need to be afraid of her."

Jenna's cheeks warmed as she realized how she must look, standing to the side and cringing as she looked at the animal in complete fear. She didn't believe a cow could be "sweet as sugar," but she also didn't want to show her nervousness in case Annie could sense it.

"I'll show you how to do it, then let you have a turn." Minnie sat down and set to work, explaining every step as she went. Jenna stood completely still, her mouth wide open in shock. Her earlier feeling of fun abruptly disappeared. She was quite certain she would never be able to drink milk from this point forward. Not to mention being able to look poor Annie in the eyes ever again.

"You look like you've just witnessed a massacre. Surely this isn't the first time you've seen a cow being milked?"

Adam's voice startled her as he came around the side of the wagon. He leaned against the wooden frame and crossed his arms over his chest.

"Well, no. I just, never really paid attention, I guess." She'd seen videos and stuff in movies but hadn't really watched closely at what was happening. And now, Adam was going to be standing here to watch her humiliation.

"All right, Jenna. Just do like I showed you and you'll be fine." Minnie stood up and let her have the stool.

Jenna inched forward, jumping when Annie lifted her head and stared at her. She had blades of grass sticking out from the sides of her mouth and Jenna was sure she was daring her to try anything with her.

"Okay, Annie. I need you to be nice. I promise this is going to be harder on me than it is on you," she whispered softly to the animal, not even caring at this point if Adam or Minnie could hear her.

She sat down and reached out for the udder,

closing her eyes as she tried to mimic the motion that Minnie had shown her.

As she squeezed, Annie mooed loudly, startling her. She quickly jumped up, falling backward over the stool. Her foot caught the pail, dumping the bit of milk that was already inside, scaring Annie in the process.

Before she even knew what was happening, Adam had his arms around her, stopping her from landing on the ground under the legs of the cow that was now jumping and kicking in confusion.

He pulled her back away from the danger and looked down into her face with a wide grin. She knew in all her life she'd never been more mortified.

"I have to say, I've done a lot in my life, but I've never had the chance to save a lady from being trampled by a cow."

She was wrong.

She was now officially more mortified.

CHAPTER 5

Jenna rolled onto her side, pulling the warm quilt up around her shoulders, careful not to wake Minnie. She was so thankful the woman had let her come with them and share everything with her. Jenna hadn't even thought about a tent or blankets, or anything like that.

But Minnie hadn't even batted an eye as they set the tent up this evening, saying there was plenty of room inside for the two of them. Charlotte was sleeping in her wagon, while Nelson and Adam would be sleeping outside.

She closed her eyes and tried to sleep, while ignoring the aching in her body. Minnie had placed a thick quilt under them to use but it wasn't much better than sleeping on the hard ground. Jenna thought about her comfortable bed back in her apartment and for the first time, wondered if she'd made a mistake.

After her performance today, it was clear everything she'd romanticized about being on the Oregon Trail was not the reality. If she couldn't even learn to milk a cow without being trampled, she wasn't going to survive. And thanks to her, they weren't going to have any butter tomorrow.

She swallowed the lump that filled her throat as she worried about what she would do. Could she see this through? Or should she just call on Dr. Lachele to come take her home.

The creaking of the wagons around them filled the evening air as people settled in for the night. Now and then, a horse would whinny, with an answering sound from one of the other animals around them. There were still a few people sitting up, and the quiet mumble of voices drifted over as they sat around their fires, possibly discussing the excitement for their futures out west.

Everyone else on this wagon train was capable of doing what they had to do in this world to survive. They surely wouldn't be scared to milk a cow.

Jenna opened her eyes, knowing she wasn't going

to be able to sleep yet, even though every bone in her body was dead tired. Carefully, she pulled the quilt back, making sure she didn't wake Minnie up as she pulled her legs out, and opened the tent flap slightly. The few remaining fires sent off a comforting glow, illuminating the other tents and wagons on the far side of the circle they'd made when they stopped.

Inside those wagons were the belongings and mementos of so many pioneers. Jenna had read so much about the Oregon Trail, and now she was able to be here to witness the hopes and dreams as these frontier people went looking for a new future.

It helped to renew her excitement, even though she knew how much hardship there would still be along the way.

SHE STEPPED OUTSIDE into the cool night air, breathing in deeply. It surprised her how clean and fresh it was out here compared to the city where she'd grown up. She wondered if it was because pollution hadn't had the chance to destroy the air here, or if it was just generally fresher outside of the city, no matter what time they were in.

It was dark on the other side of the wagons and she worried once more what would happen if she needed to "relieve" herself in the middle of the night. She would hate to have to wake Minnie up.

As it was, she was still embarrassed about the times today when they would shield each other and offer some privacy with their skirts when nature called. Just one more thing Jenna was going to have to learn to live with if she wanted to fit in here.

Annie was still grazing next to the wagon, and she lifted her head to look at Jenna. Carefully, she walked closer, making sure not to bump into the small chicken enclosure strapped onto the back of the wagon. The last thing she needed to do today was startle them and wake up the entire encampment.

She put her hand out ahead of her toward Annie's nose. The cow watched her closely, continuing to chew the food in her mouth, the crunching suddenly seeming very loud in the darkness of the night.

"Annie, I'm sorry for scaring you earlier. We're going to have to be friends because I'm determined I will learn how to milk you. I know it's incredibly degrading and most likely very uncomfortable for you, however, this is the way things are in this time. And I need to be able to fit in."

Annie just kept chewing, not really seeming interested in anything she had to say.

"You do realize that cows can't answer you, right?"

Jenna jumped, managing to stop herself from screaming as Adam spoke from behind her. She clutched at her chest as she tried to calm her racing heart.

"Why would you scare me like that? What if we'd startled poor Annie again, causing a stampede or something?"

He just shrugged, stepping closer to the cow and reaching out to scratch her under the neck. "This is where she loves to be petted. Most cows are pretty aloof, but Annie has always loved attention."

Jenna raised an eyebrow. "I'm not really sure I believe you. I'm quite sure she wasn't enjoying my attention earlier."

He laughed and motioned for her to pet Annie. "You just startled her. Trust me. Once she trusts you, she'll be your best friend."

Jenna wasn't sure if she could believe him or not, but she wasn't going to admit to him that she was terrified of a cow. Slowly she put her hand out again, and Annie stopped chewing long enough to sniff at her fingers. She held her breath as she tentatively scratched at Annie's neck. The cow lifted her head like she'd done for Adam, letting her touch the surprisingly soft fur beneath.

"I can't believe I'm touching a cow." She chuckled and grinned up at Adam.

"Well, you did technically touch her already today."

Her smile faded and she rolled her eyes as Annie leaned into her hand, letting her continue scratching. "I think the proper thing would be to not bring that up anymore."

"You're likely right. But I also likely won't listen. That's a sight I'm never going to forget, so it would be silly not to ever talk about it again."

She could only imagine the sight it had been.

After all the commotion, Charlotte had come out of her wagon, and Nelson had come from where he'd been visiting with a neighbor to see what all the ruckus was about. So, not only had Minnie and Adam witnessed her humiliation, most of the people in the wagon train probably got a glimpse too.

And, for some reason, having Charlotte snicker at what had happened had angered Jenna more than anyone else. At least Jenna had tried, and not hid in the wagon pretending to have a headache.

"Well, I'm glad I can offer you amusement at my

expense." She continued to pet Annie, not wanting to look at him.

"I'm sorry. I promise not to bring it up again." He laughed and raised his hands in surrender. "It was just nice to have something amusing to end a tiring day, and I guess I didn't consider how it might be embarrassing for you."

Jenna wasn't really too mad. She was used to doing things that might be a little more clumsy than most, so over the years, falling in front of people had become less embarrassing.

She wasn't sure why this one bothered her more.

"Now that you and Annie are friends, I would predict that the morning milking will go much smoother."

Jenna groaned and scrunched her face up as she looked at him. "Do you think your mother will make me try again already?"

"Oh, I have no doubt about it. One thing about my ma is that she never lets you give up until you've learned how to do something. That's why I'm likely the only man in the world who can mend my own socks." He dramatically looked around them. "But don't you ever tell anyone that, or I'll deny it."

She laughed, enjoying the new side of him that wasn't so grumpy all the time.

"I want to thank you for letting me join you and your mother for this trip. I know we didn't meet under the best circumstances, but I appreciate you not leaving me there."

He shrugged, reaching out to scratch the other side of Annie's neck. The cow was clearly enjoying the attention, lifting her neck and closing her eyes to get the full enjoyment of the moment.

"I might not always be considered much of a gentleman, but I'm not the kind of man to abandon a woman in need."

Suddenly, the air seemed heavier around them. She stepped back and laughed nervously, wiping her hands on her skirt.

"Well, I should turn in. It's going to be an early morning, and I need to make sure I'm ready for Annie." She smiled and kept backing toward her tent, hoping he wouldn't see how flustered she was feeling.

As she turned, she slammed into the chest of someone who had just walked around the corner of the wagon, and she let out a small scream.

"Whoa, I didn't mean to startle you, Miss Hart. I saw you and Adam over here with Annie, so I wanted to make sure you were all right after your earlier incident."

Closing her eyes against the embarrassment that hit her again, she tried to smile up at Nelson.

"I'm fine, Mr. Kent. Thank you for your concern. Mr. Wallace was kind enough to show me how gentle Annie really is, so hopefully tomorrow will be much better."

If one more person brought up the "earlier incident," she was going to find a hole to crawl into and die.

As she crouched down to slide back into the tent, she was sure she could hear the men chuckling. Well, if they wanted to have a laugh at her expense, that was completely fine.

She would show them how much she really didn't care what they thought about her.

But, as she carefully climbed back under the quilt, she knew that for a reason she didn't want to think about too much, she already cared entirely too much what one of them did.

And it wasn't the one she was sure she'd been sent here to find.

CHAPTER 6

"So, has she mentioned where she came from? I know Charlotte has a lot of questions about her. She doesn't trust her, but I think she seems quite extraordinary. I mean, we only met her today, but she's quite intriguing, wouldn't you say? I thought she handled herself well after almost being trampled by Annie." Nelson chuckled and shook his head, watching as Jenna disappeared into the tent.

Adam didn't like how the other man was looking at her, but then he silently chastised himself. Nelson was a bachelor and if he had an interest in Jenna, there would be nothing standing in his way.

But that didn't mean Adam wouldn't be keeping a close eye on him to make sure he didn't do anything improper.

"Miss Hart hasn't said much, other than she's from New York and is going west for a new life. I don't think it's our place to ask any questions until she's ready to answer."

Nelson was still looking to where she had disappeared to. "No, I guess not. I'm going to have plenty of time to get to know her before the end of the trip." He finally turned and looked at Adam. "I don't think I've ever seen eyes that blue on a woman with such striking red hair."

Adam nodded in agreement, uncomfortable to be talking about her like this. But he would have to be blind not to have seen her beauty. The strange part was, it wasn't the kind of beauty he normally noticed in a woman.

For years, he'd believed Charlotte was the most stunning woman in the world with her black hair always perfectly held up in combs, and her white skin without flaws.

Yet, Jenna's unruly hair tumbling around her shoulders tonight, and the smattering of freckles he'd noticed on her nose as she'd crinkled it in disgust when she'd tried to milk Annie, had completely enthralled him.

Adam walked back to the small fire where he'd laid his bedroll, and sat down to take off his boots, no longer wanting to discuss Miss Hart. Nelson followed, stretching before he sat on his own.

"You know, Charlotte is starting to get quite annoyed that you don't seem to appreciate her giving everything up to come out here with you. I think she'd expected a proposal by now."

Adam rested his arm on his bent knee, staring at the man across the fire.

"Well, to be honest, I had hoped to go out west on my own. I told her that from the beginning. She never showed me any attention over the years, until my uncle died, and I said I was leaving town. So, she's just going to have to wait until I'm ready." He didn't add the "if ever," figuring her brother wouldn't be too happy to hear that.

"When we get to Oregon, she wants to have her own dress shop in my new mercantile. She thinks it will be something the women out there might be lacking. So, obviously, once she's married, you'll need to offer some money toward that to get her started."

Adam turned to lay his head back on his bed, stretching his legs out on top of the blanket. "Charlotte is free to do as she pleases. If we do end up marrying, I will discuss the possibilities then. Not before. The first thing I need to focus on is getting us all to Oregon alive. I'm not sure if you noticed, but it's not going to be easy going."

He was not in the mood to discuss Charlotte. There was a time when he'd have been thrilled that she was paying him this kind of attention, and maybe he was just paying her back for all the years she ignored him. He was sure they would likely end up marrying eventually.

But for some reason, as he closed his eyes to try and sleep, instead of the black haired beauty he'd always believed was the perfect woman for him, he saw a woman with red hair, falling into his arms and staring up at him with eyes that he knew were going to haunt his dreams.

"THIS IS DISGUSTING. Surely, we could walk out a ways and find some trees, so we could have wood to use for the fire. I refuse to touch this stuff." Charlotte had her nose scrunched up and she was shaking her head as they walked along the path.

Jenna tried not to let anyone see the laugh she was trying to hold in as she bent down to pick up another piece of the buffalo poop. Of course, she was careful to call it "chips," as was proper for this time period, but in her mind, she called it like it was.

"Charlotte, on days like this, when there isn't any wood close by, we have to make do. If you can find the ones that aren't too fresh, but not too old, they're the best kind." Minnie was picking up the "perfect" piece to show Charlotte.

Jenna couldn't hold her laughter back anymore when she saw the look on Charlotte's face. Minnie turned to look at her, then started to chuckle too.

"I guess I take my buffalo chips a bit too seriously, don't I?"

The women continued walking, with Charlotte sighing loudly now and then to make sure they all knew how annoyed she was at the task they were performing.

As they walked, Jenna looked around at the wide-open ground before them. It seemed like the trail ahead of them reached up to meet the sky in the distance. She'd never seen so much open space in all her life, and it was breathtaking.

Over the past few days, everyone in the wagon train had settled into a good routine. They were up before the sun, having breakfast, and heading out while the day was still cool. After stopping for lunch and to let the animals rest, they would travel a few more hours before packing up for the evening.

So far, they'd managed to camp near water each night, so she was able to wash quickly. But she desperately wanted a bath. Somehow, she needed to sneak her shampoo with her to the water so she could give her hair a good scrub.

And she wondered why she'd even bothered to bring her e-reader with her. There was never going to be a chance to get away on her own to read it, and she wasn't sure she was ready to try explaining to anyone where she was really from. If they saw any of her "modern day" items, she worried what they might think.

"May I walk with you, please? My pa says my questions are giving him a headache."

Jenna smiled down at the young girl who had run over to them from a wagon a couple back from theirs. She'd seen her running around the camp with some of the other children, but she wasn't sure she'd ever met her parents yet.

"Your hair is just as red as mine. And you have freckles too!"

Jenna laughed and nodded. "I do. But mine aren't quite as beautiful as yours are."

She knew as a kid how much she'd hated her

freckles. So, if this little girl had ever felt the same way, Jenna wanted to make sure she knew how beautiful her freckles made her.

"My name is Mary. That's my pa over there." She waved her arm back toward the wagon she'd come from.

"Well, it's very nice to meet you, Mary. My name is Mrs. Wallace, and this is Miss Hart and Miss Kent." Minnie came over closer to do the introductions, smiling warmly at the girl.

"I'm happy to have other girls to talk to. My pa doesn't talk much. And when he does, it's just about boring stuff."

"What about your ma?"

As soon as she asked the question, Jenna could see the sadness reflected in the eyes looking back at her.

"I don't have a ma. She died."

Jenna wanted to wrap her in her arms and tell her everything would be okay.

"I don't have one either. I'm sorry about your ma, it's hard to not have one, isn't it? Sometimes, though, you can find other people who will love and care for you just the same. I know your pa must love you fiercely."

Her mind went to the friends she'd left in New

York. None of them had any parents, so they'd all been the support they needed for each other. She'd had many foster parents, and some of them hadn't been too bad, but it was sometimes hard to remember them with the memories of the worst taking over.

Mary skipped ahead, stopping now and then to pick flowers that hadn't been trampled along the path.

"I need to lie down for a spell. I can't take much more of this dust getting into my nose."

Charlotte walked ahead, staying alongside Adam for a while as he led the team. Jenna ignored the lurch in her chest at the sight of them together.

Over the past couple of days, she'd enjoyed talking with Nelson and getting to know him. But she wondered why she wasn't feeling any of the "magic" she'd been sure she was supposed to feel when she met him. She kept telling herself it would come with time.

He seemed to be quite a gentleman, and entirely different from the man she'd left behind.

But she also knew that men could hide the worst side of themselves until it was too late. So, she wasn't going to be in any hurry to let the guard down around her heart.

Her eyes stayed on Adam as Charlotte finally walked ahead to her own wagon. The jealousy she was feeling didn't make sense to her. This man wasn't her soul mate. There's no way Dr. Lachele would have sent her to someone who already belonged to someone else.

"I worry about him. He's working too hard, and Nelson doesn't seem to be able to help him much with any of the harder jobs. I know we're only a few days into our journey, but I can see the tiredness in his eyes when we stop at night."

Minnie came right up beside her, keeping her eyes on Adam too. Jenna's cheeks burned with embarrassment, knowing she'd witnessed her staring at her son.

"Hopefully once we get farther along the trail, he'll be able to relax a little bit more. I'm sure the burden of making sure we all get to Oregon is weighing on him."

Guilt washed over Jenna, knowing she'd added even more stress by tagging along. Not only to him, but to Minnie too. The older woman was still having to spend all her time teaching Jenna so much about how to cook, bake bread on the trail, even just making coffee. Something that was so simple back home, was a huge task out here.

She hadn't asked Jenna to milk Annie again, probably not wanting to waste any more milk. Of course, Charlotte had come along to learn the next day and had done it perfectly. Jenna tried not to grit her teeth.

Everything Charlotte did out here seemed to be perfect. She could cook—when she wasn't too tired or lying down with a headache. She had been helping Minnie mend clothes in the evening when needed. And she always looked completely unfrazzled and put together, even though they were in the middle of nowhere with no amenities.

Jenna just couldn't understand how a woman like Charlotte, who seemed to be so disagreeable on the one hand, could be so perfect at everything she touched on the other.

Meanwhile, Jenna seemed to burn every bit of food she tried to cook. And the one time she'd tried to help with the mending, she'd pricked her finger so badly, it bled onto the pants she'd been holding. Plus, the whole Annie incident was still quite raw in her mind.

She sometimes felt like she was more in the way than she was helping anyone.

But she was determined to keep trying. However, she'd decided if she hadn't learned enough to carry her weight on this trip, she'd try calling on Dr. Lachele to see if she could maybe go somewhere else. Surely, she wasn't stuck here if this wasn't where she was meant to be, was she?

As her gaze found the broad shoulders leading the wagon ahead of them, she found herself wishing that for once in her life, she could know without a doubt she belonged.

CHAPTER 7

*A*dam lifted the heavy yoke off the animals and set it off to the side. They'd stopped near a sheltered bit of land that had a clear stream running close by. He was grateful for the days like this, knowing there would be plenty of water and grazing for the animals because as they made it farther along the trail, there would be days they'd go without.

As soon as the animals were taken care of, he was heading to the stream to wash some of the dust and dirt off himself. It had been a grueling few days getting used to life on the trail but so far, everything had seemed to go fairly smoothly. He wasn't too naive to know that it would stay like that for the rest of the trip but as long as he got everyone there safely, that's what mattered.

He walked over toward the back of the wagon to grab a bar of soap and a cloth, and as he rounded the corner, he collided with Miss Hart whose arms were full of pots and food for their supper. He reached out to grab onto her shoulders to steady her before she could fall backward.

"Oh, I'm sorry, Mr. Wallace. I didn't see you coming."

"I can see that. You're carrying too much at once. Where are Charlotte and my mother?"

"Well, Minnie is handing me the stuff from the back of the wagon to carry over, and I think Charlotte went down to have a wash."

He wasn't surprised. It seemed like Charlotte was only ever around for the easy work.

"And I'm going to ask you to please call me, Adam. We're going to be spending weeks together out here, so we may as well forget the formalities."

She laughed, and he couldn't help smiling.

"Okay, that would be much easier for me. And you can call me Jenna. I hate being called Miss Hart. It makes me feel like an old lady."

He chuckled as he reached out to take the top few items she was precariously holding. "I would assume you'd be used to being called that. As far as I know, ladies have been addressed like that for as long as I've been alive."

She shrugged, and he noticed her cheeks redden. He was once again struck with the feeling that she was hiding something.

"Well, yes, I guess I'm used to it, but I just don't really like it."

He walked over and set the pot down on the ground, then helped her set the rest down. "If you want to go down to the stream and wash up, I can help mother get the rest of the food and utensils out of the wagon."

She shook her head as she turned to go back for another armful. "It's fine. I can help get everything going, then quickly run down after we've eaten." They rounded back behind the wagon where he could hear things being moved around inside.

"Oh, Adam. I'm glad you're here. You can set our tent out for us to set up." His mother flung the canvas into his arms before handing a container of flour to Jenna.

As they walked back over to where they were setting up their camp, Jenna looked around. "Where is Nelson? I never see him around too much when we first stop for the evening."

A pang of jealousy hit him before he could shake

it off. He just shrugged and clenched his jaw from saying what he really wanted to say about the man. He'd known Nelson all his life and knew he wasn't much for manual labor, but he'd thought by now the man would realize he had to pitch in and help more. Instead, he went off to socialize, while Adam took care of the livestock and the women prepared supper.

He'd always had everyone do things for him and just expected it out here too.

"He likes to visit with some of the other travelers. Likely making sure he can drum up business when he gets to Oregon."

Adam knew Nelson had caught the eye of a couple of single ladies in their outfit. But he didn't think Jenna needed to know he was out flirting with other women when he wasn't here showering his attentions on her. Every night, Adam had to sit and listen to the man brag to her about how successful he'd been when he took over his father's mercantile.

He was sure before long; Jenna would be completely enthralled with the man. He had a lot to offer her.

"Adam, I'm just going around to make sure everyone knows we will be stopping here for the day tomorrow. We're making good time, so we'll take a day to rest the animals."

Adam turned to see the captain of the outfit standing by the wagon just as his mother walked over.

"Oh, that will be perfect. We can wash some clothes and give them a chance to dry. And I must say, I will enjoy a day to give my poor aching feet a rest too."

"Mother, I don't think you've properly met our captain. Luke, this is my mother, Mrs. Mary Wallace, and this lady beside her is Miss Jenna Hart." He stepped aside so they could properly meet the man he was introducing. "Ladies, this is Mr. Luke Bryan, the captain of our little outfit."

Jenna's eyes widened and her mouth opened in surprise as she chuckled softly. Did she know him already?

"Mr. Luke Bryan? That's your real name?"

Adam had talked with Luke many times over the past few days and he was the perfect one to lead them west. He was honest and fair, but he also didn't take guff from anyone. And now he was staring at Jenna with an eyebrow raised in confusion.

"That's my name, ma'am."

Even under her bonnet, Adam could see her

cheeks redden. He had no idea why she was so shocked to hear his name, but she obviously had realized they were all watching her.

"I'm sorry. It's just that a friend of mine used to know someone with that name. It just startled me to hear it. I'm sorry if I was being rude."

Luke shrugged and chuckled before starting to walk to the next wagon. "Well, I'm quite certain the other Luke Bryan could never be anywhere near as handsome as this one."

As the captain walked away, laughing at his own joke, he stopped to talk to another man who was walking over with a young girl beside him. Adam was starting to get annoyed at seeing just how many men were hanging around his wagon all of a sudden.

"Oh, Miss Mary. I'm so happy to see you again." His mother reached out to take the little girl's hand. Adam recognized her as the girl who had been walking with them earlier.

The man walked over and stood by them. "I wanted to thank you for letting Mary walk with you ladies today. I sure appreciate it. She's finding the time a bit long having just me for company."

"It's no trouble at all. Mary is welcome to join us any time she wants." Jenna smiled down at the girl.

The man put his hand out toward Adam. "Name's Hunter McQuaid."

Adam shook his hand and introduced his mother and Jenna too. With the amount of time everyone in this wagon train would be spending together over the weeks ahead, he was sure they'd all become quite well acquainted by the end of the trip.

But, while both Hunter and the captain looked to be nice enough men, he'd be quite happy if they weren't around all the time.

And it wasn't at all because he was feeling any jealousy about Jenna.

"You and Mary are welcome to stay and have supper with us. We have plenty of food, and tonight should be a celebration shared with new friends."

Adam cringed as his mother invited the man to stay for supper and tried not to show his disappointment when he accepted.

The women took Mary to let her help prepare the meal while he stood with Hunter.

"Mary is quite taken with Miss Hart. She's talked about her non-stop since this afternoon. She said she's never met someone so beautiful with red hair and freckles like her."

Adam watched the women who were over by the

small fire setting the bacon on the pan. Jenna was crouched down, letting Mary help her.

Suddenly, he realized there was a flame on the hem of Jenna's skirt, and she hadn't noticed.

"Jenna!" He ran over and pulled her back from the fire, quickly patting at the fabric to stop the flames from spreading. He was still holding onto her arm when he looked up and saw the look of shock on her face.

Before she could look away, he watched her eyes fill with tears, but she quickly put her head down and wiped at her skirt as she backed away.

"Oh, my goodness. I'm so clumsy, I guess I didn't realize how close I was to the fire." She lifted her head and smiled apologetically at everyone who had gathered around her in concern.

"I will go change my skirt and be right back."

She turned to walk to the wagon with her head held high and shoulders back, but not before he'd seen the look of complete embarrassment in her eyes.

Since the day she'd arrived, she'd been trying so hard to prove she wasn't an extra burden. He might be a man, but he could understand when a woman would be feeling like she wasn't measuring up. He remembered feeling like nothing he did was right when he was first learning the blacksmith trade from his uncle.

His uncle had just kept reminding him that everything took time to learn and the only way to do it was to keep messing it up.

Adam had no doubt that Jenna would figure it all out, because one thing she had more than anyone else he'd ever met, was the determination to try.

CHAPTER 8

"Supper was delicious. And the coffee was the best I've had in days." Hunter stood up and walked over to Jenna, reaching down for the sleeping girl in her arms. "I'm sorry if she's bothered you at all. She's really been missing her ma, and I think she sees a bit of her in you."

Jenna smiled as she stood up to hand Mary to her father. "It's fine. She hasn't bothered me at all. It's nice to have someone you can feel safe with, so if I can give her that, then it would make me very happy."

It had been a wonderful evening, relaxing and visiting with their neighboring travelers. Everyone was happy, knowing they wouldn't have to be up at the crack of dawn to move out. She could hear a violin and singing at a wagon farther down, while others had chosen to go to bed early and enjoy the chance to catch up on sleep.

As he walked away, she thought to herself that Hunter was a nice man. She'd noticed he was a bit evasive when asked about his late wife, or what his plans were when he made it out west, but Jenna knew what it was like to have secrets better left unshared, so it wasn't her place to judge.

"Supper was delicious, Charlotte. Your biscuits were perfect."

Jenna sat back down on the crate and stared at the fire as Nelson complimented his sister. After Jenna had almost caught herself and the young girl on fire earlier, she'd retreated to the wagon to change. She had made sure to take enough time to pull herself together after the embarrassment she'd been feeling.

It wasn't a big thing that had happened, like almost getting trampled by a cow for instance, but it had highlighted her fears about not being able to do anything right out here. And it had happened in front of everyone.

By the time she'd crawled back out of the wagon bed, Charlotte was out there with her hair perfectly combed and tied in ribbons, cooking the evening meal without any trouble at all. It had just made everything sting a little bit more.

"Did you burn your leg at all, Jenna? Or was it just your skirt that got scorched?"

Jenna had been hoping the earlier incident had been forgotten but no, thanks to Charlotte, now everyone was reminded. Charlotte looked at her with fake concern, and Jenna knew for a fact she didn't really care. She just wanted to make sure everyone saw how much more adequate she was compared to the new girl.

Jenna had met many girls like Charlotte over the years, so she knew exactly what she was doing.

But Jenna *was* the new girl here. She wasn't a part of these families who had known each other for years. So, she had to play nice because no one would believe her if she called her out on it anyway.

"I'm fine. Just a little mark on my lower leg but that's all. My skirt wasn't so lucky, though." She tried to laugh it off, hoping no one would notice how uncomfortable she was that it had been brought up again.

"Oh, well if you give it to me tomorrow, I'll mend it and fix it up better than new." Charlotte was smiling, hoping everyone would appreciate her generosity. And Jenna would look like a horrible person if she told her what she was really thinking about her offer.

Jenna wanted to go over and push her off the box she was sitting on right beside Adam.

"Now, I'm going to get some sleep. It was an exhausting day walking, then making supper. I will see you in the morning." Charlotte stood up, waiting for Adam to walk her to her wagon.

Jenna fought the urge to roll her eyes as they walked off.

"And if you'll excuse me, ladies, there's a game of cards happening that I'd hate to miss out on. You can let Adam know he's welcome to join us when he's back." Nelson stood up and walked away, without even asking if anyone else might like to go. But then, Jenna figured a game of cards back in this time wasn't something a lady would be invited to.

She wasn't sure how she was ever supposed to have any time to get to know Nelson when he didn't hang around much, but she figured they had weeks ahead of them, so there wasn't any hurry.

"Don't let Charlotte get to you, Jenna. I appreciate all your help, whether you think you're helping or not." Minnie reached over and patted Jenna's leg. "She just isn't used to having another beautiful woman around to have to compete for men's attention."

Jenna laughed and rolled her eyes. "Well, there isn't any competition really. My hair looks like those tumbleweeds we saw earlier today, and I'm sure I have even more freckles than ever after these past few days."

She'd been wearing her sunscreen and trying to reapply as much as possible, but she found that if she had too much on and didn't get it rubbed in enough, it left a cake of mud stuck to her skin within a couple of hours.

"Ma, if you want to crawl into bed early, Jenna can milk Annie. I'll help her."

Adam walked back into the light of the fire, startling her when he spoke. She quickly looked at Minnie with her eyes wide, hoping the older woman would help her.

"That would be wonderful. Thank you, Jenna."

She stood up as Minnie did and looked back over at Adam, trying to keep her voice from coming out shrieky like it did when she was nervous. "But...I'm not sure...I haven't really tried again since the first time."

He just shrugged and started walking to the back where Annie was grazing, not even caring that she was about to be accosted again. Even though she'd made a point of coming over to scratch Annie's neck at least once a day, Jenna wasn't sure the cow was entirely okay with her after their first meeting.

Jenna raced to catch up to him. "Maybe you should just do it. I don't want to cause a scene here tonight, when everyone is having a nice evening relaxing."

Adam just turned and grinned at her as he pushed the little stool over toward Annie. He reached over and lifted the pail off the ground by the wagon wheel and thrust it in her direction. "No, you can do it. Annie much prefers the hands of a woman over mine."

Jenna wanted to run and just forget she'd ever thought coming to this time period would be a good idea. Wasn't it enough for him that she'd almost caught herself on fire today? Did he really need to see her further humiliation?

She sighed loudly, hoping he would get the hint at her annoyance. Annie lifted her head and looked at her suspiciously, so she stuck her hand out for her to sniff at it. "I'm sorry, sweet girl. But this man is insisting I need to try getting milk from you again. Now, I know we might not have gotten off on the right foot before, but I promise I will do my best not to hurt you. Although, I admit, it looks like this task has to be incredibly painful for you."

She knew she was babbling now as she tried to avoid the job, and Adam was standing back with his arms crossed, trying not to laugh as she spoke. "I appreciate that you're being so thoughtful to Annie's feelings, but again, I can assure you, she doesn't understand a word you're saying."

"Well, I know that. But if you speak with a soothing voice, they're less likely to want to kill you." She shot him an annoyed look, hoping Annie couldn't sense her frustration.

She sat on the stool and closed her eyes, speaking softly to Annie to explain exactly what she was doing. She went through the motions she'd remembered Minnie teaching her, still too scared to open her eyes.

"That's it, Jenna. You're doing it." Adam's voice came from just beside her ear, so she knew he had to be hunched over watching her closely. But before she could let herself get too stressed about that fact, she heard the sound of milk squirting into the bucket.

She quickly opened her eyes and looked up at Adam, grinning. "I actually got milk out!" she whispered loudly, not wanting to startle Annie now that the cow was being nice enough to stand still for her.

Adam was grinning too as he nodded for her to keep going.

If she'd ever thought two months ago she'd be giddy with excitement over sitting in the dark milking a cow in the middle of nowhere, she would have thought she was going crazy.

But right now, it felt like the weight of a hundred milk cows had been lifted from her shoulders. Now, she needed to just finish the job without actually spilling anything, and then she could celebrate her win.

"There, now was that so hard?" When she was finished and had drained the last of the milk from the udder, Adam finally spoke again as he reached out to pick up the pail.

"Well, it's much easier when the cow isn't trying to kill you." She followed him over to the wagon where they could strain it into the little buckets before covering it for the night.

He helped her finish, then turned to face her. She smiled at him, suddenly feeling the darkness of the night around them. It felt like they were the only people still awake, but she knew that wasn't true.

She could hear the voices and laughter of others still up enjoying the evening.

"Thank you for making me do this."

He shrugged nonchalantly, still with a wide grin on his face. Even in the fading light, his smile took her breath away.

"I knew you'd be able to do it. And the longer you put off trying again, the harder it was going to be."

"I know I'm a bit clumsy out here, but everything is just so different than what I'm used to back home. I'm having to relearn everything."

He leaned against the wagon again and looked at her intently.

"Whenever you talk about back home, it always sounds so mysterious. I know it's none of my concern, and you can tell me it's none of my business, but are you really from New York? I feel like there's more you aren't saying about where you're from, or what you're running away from."

She swallowed and looked down at his boots. "I am from New York. Maybe someday I can tell you everything, but for now, I'll just tell you that I'm running away from someone who has decided if he can't have me, no one else can. And if he has his way, he'll make sure no one does."

When she looked up, Adam was scowling down at her. "What do you mean? A man is trying to hurt you?" He hesitated, then dropped his voice, "A husband?"

She shook her head, hoping she wasn't telling him too much. This was the kind of stuff she should be talking about with Nelson as she got to know him, not Adam.

"No, just a man who I know is capable of causing me physical harm. He's done it before."

Adam's eyes filled with anger. The muscles in his jaw moved as he clenched it tight. "Well, I give you my word that as long as you're in my care, he won't find you or ever lay a hand on you. And if he tries, he will answer to me."

As she stood there feeling the intensity of his anger, for the first time in her life, she truly believed she had someone who would protect her with everything they had.

CHAPTER 9

*A*dam had spent the morning making minor repairs on their wagons and helping out fellow travelers with theirs. Everyone wanted to make sure things were ready for the next long leg of the journey. Luke had said they'd stop now and then for a rest day, as long as they continued at a good pace. But there were no guarantees of when those days would be, so everyone had to be ready.

"I'm heading down to the stream to see if the ladies need a hand carrying the washing back. Would you like to join me?"

Adam looked up from where he was working to see Nelson standing there looking like he'd just stepped out of the tailors. His pants didn't even seem to have a wrinkle in them and were a stark contrast to the dirty pants Adam wore. How could the man be out here in these conditions and never look like he had a speck of dust on him?

"Sure, I'll grab some soap and wash up while I'm down there. I'll wait and go down for a nice refreshing bath later when the ladies aren't present."

"I'd thought of doing the same. And I suppose we should offer some opportunity of privacy for the womenfolk to have the chance too. I'd hate to think anyone might take advantage and try to sneak a peek, though."

Adam nodded in agreement. "Well, we can sit guard and make sure they get some time without any interruption once they've got the washing hung up to dry back at camp."

Along the embankment, the women of the wagon train worked tirelessly, laughing and enjoying the opportunity to socialize. Adam's eyes immediately found Jenna who was leaning right into the water, the bottom of her skirt completely drenched, as she wrung out a blouse.

His mother was working beside her, and he looked around for Charlotte. She was farther up the bank, visiting with one of the other ladies and it didn't look like her skirts were wet at all. Every bit of hair was still tucked neatly beneath her bonnet.

He almost laughed out loud when he looked back and saw Jenna with curls hanging out in every direction. She lifted her head up and noticed him, sending him a smile as she reached up and wiped at her brow.

"Well, it's nice of you to show up now that we've got everything washed already. We could have used some help wringing out some of those thick pants and dresses." She was laughing as she walked up the bank with the blouse she'd just washed to put it into the basket.

Minnie walked over and placed the apron she'd washed on top. "Good heavens. Can you imagine? Having men helping wash my bloomers?"

They laughed to themselves as they started to tidy up the items they'd used for washing the clothes. He was happy to see that Jenna had obviously managed to do this without any incident to shake her confidence again. After last night, she'd woken up early to milk Annie all on her own, and he was sure he'd never seen anyone as proud as she'd been to show them the full pail.

"While the thought of having to wash my mother's bloomers is quite likely to give me nightmares, I can assure you ladies that I was busy tending to other jobs that needed doing." He wasn't sure Nelson could say the same, but he ignored the urge to point that out.

"We came to help you carry the heavy washing back up to the wagons." He quickly bent down to grab Jenna's basket before Nelson could, leaving the other man to pick up his sister's instead. Minnie looked between the men and rolled her eyes.

"Well, I guess I'll just carry my own then. Which includes your clothes too, I might point out, Adam."

His cheeks warmed as he went over and set Jenna's basket on top of his mother's, to carry them both. The wet clothes were heavy and now having the two baskets made it awkward.

Charlotte finally walked over, offering him a sultry smile. "Adam, how nice of you to come help us carry our clothes back. I had so much to do, with Nelson's and mine. I was done a while ago but decided to go visit with some of the other ladies while your mother helped Jenna do her few bits."

His mother looked at Charlotte with a blank expression, but Adam could see she wasn't pleased with her feeling the need to point out that Jenna had needed some help.

"Well, I helped Jenna because she helped me with mine. We did all of it together." Minnie smiled warmly at Jenna.

Charlotte came over and threaded her arm through his for the walk back to the wagons and his eyes found Jenna. She was watching them closely, but when their eyes met, she quickly turned away, busying herself with picking up the soap on the ground.

Suddenly, Nelson shouted, drawing everyone's attention. By the time Adam saw him, he was on the ground holding his ankle with the basket of clothes strewn around him.

"Oh my, Mr. Kent, are you all right?"

Adam took a moment to enjoy the fact that Jenna was still using the more formal greeting for Nelson as he watched her race over to him. She crouched down next to him while Charlotte called out to her brother.

"Nelson! Are you all right?" She looked around at the clothes on the ground. "Hopefully nothing got too dirty. I don't want to have to rewash everything."

Adam set his baskets down, disentangling himself from Charlotte's arm.

"What did you do?" He looked down at the man who was wincing in pain.

"I must have stepped in a hole or something. One minute I was walking with the basket, and the next thing I know, my ankle was twisted in the wrong direction."

Jenna stood up and looked at Adam, concern evident in her face. "Can you help him stand up? He can lean on me until we get back to the wagon."

Adam thought he saw a flash of joy on the wounded man's face when he heard the suggestion, but surely, he was just imagining it.

"I can help him get back to the wagon then come back for all the baskets." Adam reached his hand out to help Nelson stand. He hopped around trying to put weight on his foot, but it was obvious he wasn't going to be able to.

Jenna let Nelson put an arm around her shoulder. She put one around his waist and let him lean on her. "Don't be silly. There's no sense making extra work for you. He can lean on me until we get back, so you can carry the baskets."

Minnie was quickly picking up the clothes and flapping the dust off them before putting them back into the basket. "I can manage with this one, Adam, if you carry the rest."

It was clear Charlotte wasn't going to offer and he couldn't keep standing here arguing with Jenna about helping Nelson. So, he followed behind the couple ahead of him, fuming every time Nelson had to limp and lean more into Jenna.

Charlotte came up beside him and put her arm through his again, making small talk as they walked back to the wagon. He was trying to listen to what she was saying but right now he was too annoyed about everything. He caught his mother's eye, but he ignored the knowing look she was giving him.

"I'm just going to lie down over by the wagon in the shade, if you can help me, Jenna." Adam thought Nelson was seriously taking advantage of his injury, wincing loudly as he tried to act brave while Jenna helped him get down on the ground.

He had to refrain from applauding the man who was putting on such a good show.

"Here, let me get a blanket for you to lean back on, and I will find something for you to elevate your foot. You should take your boot off in case it's swelling, or it might get stuck."

Jenna was fussing over Nelson, plumping his blanket behind his head, then turning to help him get his boot off.

"You really should get all these clothes hanging up or you're going to have terrible wrinkles. I'm sure Nelson will be just fine now that he's lying down."

His voice sounded grumpy, and Jenna turned to

scowl at him. "Well, a few wrinkles won't kill anyone. I can't just leave him here without making sure he's comfortable."

The way Nelson was acting, anyone who came along now would think he'd had his entire leg ripped off.

Adam didn't need to stand here and watch Jenna doting over a man who was clumsy enough to step in a hole and hurt himself. With a sinking feeling, Adam also realized it now meant he truly didn't have any help with the harder jobs around here.

Adam wasn't sure how he was supposed to drive two wagons until Nelson was well enough to walk again, which by the performance he was witnessing wouldn't be until they made it all the way to Oregon.

CHAPTER 10

"Are you sure you can do this? It's not a job for a woman. I would feel a lot safer if we found another man who could help. I could even ask Luke."

Jenna glared at Adam and shook her head. "I will be fine. It's not like these animals ever go very fast, so I highly doubt I'm going to be trampled by them. I'll just walk beside you, and if I have any trouble, you'll be right here."

She held tightly to the rope tied to the oxen, waiting for the signal to head out.

"Here, at least wear my gloves. Otherwise your hands will be nothing but blisters by the end of the day." Adam reached out and handed her the gloves he'd been wearing.

She put them on, noticing the heat still inside from his hands. "They're so big, it will be a miracle if they even stay on."

He smiled and shrugged. "At least they will protect your hands."

When the voices rang out, telling everyone it was time to move, she had a moment of panic. Why had she agreed to do this? Until a couple of weeks ago, the closest she'd ever come to a large animal was that time they went to a petting zoo and she'd been spat on by a llama.

Now, here she was milking cows and leading a team of oxen across the prairies.

"Are you sure?"

The concern in Adam's eyes and voice were almost her undoing, but she just nodded and mimicked what he was doing. He shouted out for the oxen to move, and thankfully hers listened to him too. She almost screeched when they started to walk but she had to act cool after insisting she would be able to do this.

He'd been so worried last night, and she'd seen how heavy everything was on his shoulders when Nelson informed them there was no way he could lead the oxen for a few days.

While they were fairly easy to lead, they did

require a bit of coaxing now and then. So, that was now going to be her job until Nelson's ankle was better.

She could tell it was just a bit of a sprain when he'd taken his boot and sock off, even though he was making sure everyone saw how painful it was for him. She'd sprained her ankle badly once playing soccer and had managed to hobble around just fine afterward.

Still, she thought maybe she wasn't being fair to Nelson. It was probably worse than hers had been. He certainly had seemed to be in a great deal of pain, and they hadn't been able to ice it. But seeing the weariness on Adam's face as he tried to figure out how he'd manage as the only man in their party, had left her feeling less than generous toward Nelson.

Adam was already trying to do too much. She'd noticed Nelson wasn't much help to him with the livestock or some of the other jobs, but she hoped over the weeks ahead he might do a bit more. Otherwise, she worried that Adam would collapse from exhaustion.

"Just keep your hand steady and watch your path ahead. I don't need you stepping into a hole and hurting yourself too." He smiled over at her reassuringly as they started making their way over the uneven ground. As long as she could stay close enough beside him, she wasn't as worried about anything going wrong. But it was going to be hard to hear him talking with the creaking of the wagons and the noises of the animals as they pulled the heavy load.

They walked in silence for a while as she concentrated on keeping the wagon moving. Nelson was propped up with some blankets inside, and she cringed every time they hit a hard bump. It wouldn't be comfortable for him back there but there was no way to find a smooth path out here. There weren't any.

Besides, Charlotte seemed to be managing to find it comfortable enough to ride for at least a while every day, so it couldn't be too bad.

Minnie was walking behind with Charlotte, and when Jenna peeked back, she smiled to see Mary had joined them again. She was running circles around the older women and most likely talking a mile a minute.

After a while, Luke rode up from the front of the wagons. "How are you doing, Jenna? Are you sure you can manage? I could try finding a spare hand to help out."

She shook her head. "No, I'm managing all right. Adam is right here in case anything goes wrong."

Luke nodded, then carried on to check on the others.

So far, the animals seemed to be behaving, other than the odd time she had to coax them to keep moving, so she didn't mind doing this job. Besides, it was kind of nice being up here with Adam, instead of listening to the constant loud sighs and complaining from Charlotte.

"So, what are your plans when you get to Oregon?" She looked over at Adam who she knew was keeping his wagon much closer to hers than he did when Nelson was leading it.

He smiled as he looked ahead. "I'm headed to a little town called Bethany, in the Willamette Valley, where I have family living. They're in need of a blacksmith in town, so they asked if I'd be interested in coming out. I haven't seen some of my cousins in quite a while. Colton was out east a few years back and stopped in to visit me, then led a wagon train back to Oregon."

She watched his face fill with excitement as he talked about seeing his family. "How many cousins do you have out there?"

He laughed and looked over at her. "There are

five of them. And from what I've heard, they've all been marrying and having babies, so now there'll be even more family to visit with. Plus, my aunt Anna is there. Before they moved out west, she and my mother were very close, and I know she's missed her ever since. They're both widows, so it will be nice for them to have each other."

Jenna could feel the love as he spoke about his aunt and cousins. She couldn't even imagine what it would be like to have that much extended family.

"So, is it just you and your mother? You don't have any brothers or sisters?" Jenna was always fascinated hearing about other people's families.

He turned back and looked ahead, and she noticed his face had dropped slightly. "I had a brother, but he died when he was twelve. I was older than him, and he got sick with pneumonia. I'd always been the big brother doing my best to protect him but..." He shrugged and let the rest of the sentence hang in the air.

"You don't feel guilty for not being able to save him, do you? There's nothing you could have done."

"I know that logically. But part of me still feels like I let him down. I know it's maybe silly, but as a kid, it's easy to take those burdens onto your own shoulders."

She tried to picture Adam as a young boy himself, heartbroken over losing his brother and taking the guilt of not protecting him, letting it weigh him down. No wonder he took his job of protecting everyone in his care so seriously now.

"It must have been pretty hard on your mom too."

He looked at her sideways, and she cringed when she realized she'd used the word mom. That wasn't a common way to address a parent in this time, and she'd been trying hard to watch how she spoke to fit in better.

But he just nodded, then looked back to where Minnie was laughing with Mary.

"It was. She took it hard. She'd already lost a baby girl shortly after she was born, and then my pa died a year after my brother. So, she's had a rough time, but still keeps smiling and showing a strength I haven't seen in many other people."

"Your mother is a pretty amazing woman. She's exactly how I would have pictured my own mother to be, if I'd known her."

She watched as Minnie pretended to chase Mary. The little girl was squealing with happiness, while Charlotte stayed back away from them. Jenna knew it wouldn't be long before she was too tired and needed to rest.

"You never knew your mother?" He was looking at her intently, and she suddenly felt the emotions come rushing forward as she always did. She hated that people pitied her when they found out she was an orphan—without any family who had ever claimed her.

"No. I never knew any of my family. I was left on the steps of a church in the middle of New York City, and no one ever came forward to claim me." She shrugged and pretended it didn't bother her as much as it did. "I never had a family."

"So, did you grow up in an orphanage?"

Jenna pretended to busy herself with keeping the oxen moving, giving herself some time to think of her answer. She had no idea if foster care was a "thing" back in this time, so as a baby with no family, she probably would have lived in an orphanage.

"Well, not really. A few families took turns taking me in and caring for me until I was old enough to live on my own."

How else could she explain the foster care system to him? She'd been one of the "unadoptable" ones. She never knew why no one wanted to adopt her, and over the years as she got older, her chances got slimmer, so she became very bitter.

She peeked over at him to see if he believed her, and he was scowling and shaking his head. "That doesn't sound like a great way for a child to grow up. I'm sorry you had to live like that."

She shrugged nonchalantly, not wanting to let him see just how hard it had been for her. "I ended up being a pretty angry child, so I probably didn't make it any easier for myself. I acted out a lot. I'm sure most of the families were doing their best to look after me."

"Acted out? Like in the theater?" He gave her a puzzled look.

She inwardly groaned. Another lost in translation from another century moment.

Suddenly, a loud crack of thunder sounded in the distance, startling the oxen and causing them to stop. It had been overcast all day, with clouds hovering, but now the first few drops of rain could be felt on her skin just as a slight wind started to blow.

"Will we stop for the storm?" Jenna hoped he couldn't see how nervous the heavy, black clouds ahead of them were making her as she pulled and got the oxen moving again.

"Depends how bad it looks. Luke will have to

decide if he thinks there's any danger. It's best to be stopped with the livestock corralled if things start to get bad."

He was looking ahead to see if the order had been given to stop. Before they had a chance to figure it out, the sky opened, and the rain fell so hard, Jenna could barely see him. He reached out for her rope, yelling for her to get back into the wagon.

"No, I'll help you get them unhooked from the wagons. You can't do it by yourself."

She had to yell to be heard over the pounding rain. All around them, other wagons were moving into the circle formation, so she continued pulling hers, falling in behind Adam's.

When they stopped, he rushed over and lifted the yoke off the oxen, throwing it off to the side. He slapped the first one on the hind end, coaxing them all into the middle. "There. Now get in the wagon before you get hurt."

She could tell this time he wasn't taking no for an answer, so she ran back to climb in after Minnie. As she ran past Annie, still tied to the side of the wagon, she wanted to stop and offer her new friend some reassuring words, but by the look on the cow's face, she wasn't bothered by the weather at all.

Before she climbed in, she took one last look to

see Adam struggling to unhitch the other team. She wished she could be more help to him, but she knew she would just be in his way.

If Nelson truly was the man she was sent here for, Jenna wondered when she'd start seeing a side of him that would make her want to be with him.

Because as she watched Adam working so hard in the pouring rain, to make sure everything was taken care of, Jenna wasn't feeling much affection for the man sitting nice and dry in his own wagon.

CHAPTER 11

*A*dam sat on the overturned crate, waiting for the coffee to finish heating up. He didn't know if he would ever completely dry out but as he watched the other travelers moving around their wagons, he realized he wasn't the only one soaked through to the skin.

The rain hadn't lasted long, but it was enough to make the ground muddy and treacherous. Luke had made the call to stay camped until morning to let everyone get dried out and hopefully by tomorrow, it would be easier going.

By the time he'd finished getting everything secured in the rain, and checked on Charlotte and Nelson, he'd been drenched. When he'd climbed into the wagon with his mother and Jenna, there hadn't been much room to spare. With all their provisions and belongings packed in, the women were already sitting precariously on trunks and barrels.

He'd ended up right next to Jenna, and he hated to admit how nice it had felt being that close to her. He knew he likely should have gotten in with Charlotte, but she had Nelson to look after her, and he had wanted to make sure he was there in case his mother needed him.

He told himself it had nothing to do with the fact Jenna had been in that wagon too.

Guilt was gnawing at his insides, knowing he was responsible for Charlotte, and that she'd given everything up to come west with him. It didn't matter that he hadn't asked her to. The fact she was here and had the intention that she'd be marrying him when they got to Oregon, left him feeling empty.

It wasn't what he wanted, but it wasn't fair to her if he didn't. He had an obligation, so regardless of the feelings he was fighting for Jenna, he was going to have to follow through. He wasn't the kind of man to abandon a woman, especially one he'd spent most of his life expecting to marry.

He should be excited. He should have been insisting they marry before they even got to Oregon.

But he hadn't. And that wasn't even something he could blame on Jenna. He realized now he hadn't really wanted to marry Charlotte. It had been something he'd thought he wanted as a young man, but once he'd made that decision to come west, he knew she wasn't a part of that future.

And now, he had no choice but to do right by her.

His mother lifted the pot off the fire and poured him a cup. "You should go change into dry clothes or you'll end up with pneumonia. I don't know why you insist on being so stubborn."

He laughed as he took a sip of the warm coffee. "Because I'm just like my mother." He took pity on her and offered her a reassuring smile. "I'll be fine, Ma. I won't get pneumonia." He knew she always worried so much about him ending up sick like his brother, so he reached out and squeezed her hand.

"Besides, I think there's someone else you should be more worried about." He nodded his head toward where Jenna was standing and petting Annie, leaning in and talking into her ear. She'd taken such a liking to that animal, it seemed like every time he looked, she was over there doting on her. And Annie was loving the attention. He laughed and shook his head. Why did she think that animal could understand her?

Jenna's dress was soaked through and had to weigh twice what it normally did, yet there she stood, soothing a cow who most likely hadn't even been truly bothered by the storm anyway.

"Oh, that was terrifying. I hope we don't ever have another storm like that." Charlotte emerged from her wagon, completely changed into a dry dress and her hair neatly combed, tied up in clips perfectly around her face.

He almost laughed out loud when he looked to see Jenna walking toward them with her matted wet hair hanging limply down over her shoulders, dripping water onto her already soaked clothing. But she didn't seem to care at all and smiled at them all warmly. "Well, Annie is fine, so that's good."

This time, he did laugh at the look of disbelief on Charlotte's face when she looked at Jenna. "You're still walking around in your wet dress? Worrying about a cow?" Charlotte shook her head then went over to assist Nelson who was stepping out of the wagon.

The man limped over to an empty crate and plunked down, wincing to make sure everyone saw how much pain he was in.

"I'm going to start frying up some bacon. Jenna, you get in that wagon and change into dry clothes.

Charlotte, you can help me carry everything over here to get started."

"But I was hoping to have just a few minutes to sit and rest. That storm was frightening. And besides, I'm barely dry."

Jenna walked to the back of the wagon with his mother. "I can help you get everything out before I get changed. A few more minutes of being soaked won't hurt anyway."

"No, get in there and get some dry clothes on. I'll help her." Adam stood up, brushing past Charlotte to help his mother carry the pans and food back to the fire. He wasn't in the mood to listen to Charlotte's excuses, but when she realized he was helping, she quickly came to offer a hand too.

They took the items Jenna handed out of the wagon, then she pulled the canvas closed behind her. He could see the wagon shaking as she tried to maneuver in the tight space to get the wet clothes off. It wouldn't be an easy task compared to taking off dry clothing that didn't stick everywhere. When he heard a loud crash of something falling, then her mumbled voice he almost thought was speaking some very unladylike words, he wondered if she could manage without breaking anything. He smiled to himself as he walked back to the fire.

"Jenna seemed to manage all right, didn't she? It was a bit bumpy in spots, but at least the wagon stayed on the path. I was a bit worried when the storm started that the team would bolt with me in the back."

Nelson reached out to take the offered cup of coffee from Minnie, while Adam sat back down next to him.

"She did all right. Hopefully your ankle will be better before too long, so she won't have to continue doing it. Especially since it's likely going to be rough going tomorrow on the muddy ground, and Luke says we have a river crossing coming up in a couple of days. I'm going to need your help with that. There's no way Jenna can do it."

"How are we going to get across the river?" Charlotte looked over at him with a concerned look as she placed the bacon onto the pan. More guilt hit him as he realized the danger they were all in with every day on this trail, and if anything happened to her, it was his fault for allowing her to come.

"It's not a big crossing, this time. But there will be some risks, so I'll need everyone helping. Hopefully everything will go smoothly, and we won't lose anything." He didn't add the "or anyone" that flashed into his mind.

He would never forgive himself if anything happened to any of them.

As he watched the woman now crawling out of the back of the wagon, catching the hem of her dress on her boot and almost falling onto the ground, he swallowed hard.

Jenna gave him a warm smile as she walked over to them at the fire.

And he realized that if anything happened to her, he was quite sure his heart would never recover. He'd only known her for a short time, but he could see he was dangerously close to falling in love with this woman, who was nothing like the woman he thought he wanted to marry.

The woman he was obligated to marry.

Even if his heart belonged to someone else.

CHAPTER 12

"We can get both of your wagons across, with Mary riding over with Miss Hart and your mother, then we can come back over for my rig."

Hunter was sitting with Adam as they prepared the wagons to make the river crossing. Jenna was washing the dishes from breakfast, with Mary beside her drying. Since Nelson's ankle was still in a great deal of pain, he didn't think he'd be able to help much.

He'd have to ride across in one of the wagons with the women. Where most men would likely be upset at the prospect of not being able to do the "manly" work, Nelson seemed perfectly fine with the arrangement.

"Will it be dangerous going through the water? What if the animals drown?" Mary had been asking Jenna a hundred questions this morning, obviously quite worried about the day ahead.

And Jenna didn't have the answers. She was just as nervous about the prospect of having to cross the river that Luke had said wasn't "that bad." He'd said there would be much worse crossings ahead, which terrified Jenna. She'd gone down to the river last night when they'd arrived and had already noticed how fast it was flowing.

If this was considered easy, she was not prepared for any of the worse ones.

"We'll all be fine, Mary. Don't you worry. Your pa and Adam will make sure we all make it across safely. I'm sure it's not even that deep." Every word she spoke to the little girl was trying to assure herself too.

Adam heard them talking and smiled over at the young girl. "Don't worry, Mary. Miss Hart is strong enough to pull the oxen through the water to the other side on her own, so we don't have anything to worry about."

Jenna shot an eyebrow up as she fought the urge to roll her eyes at him. Just because she'd been able to lead the team over some muddy ground the past couple of days, didn't mean she was strong enough to drag them all through the river.

But she did appreciate his confidence, even if he was exaggerating terribly.

"Well, Miss Hart won't be doing anything like that at all. She will most likely be sitting in the back of the wagon with her head buried in a blanket until it's all over." She smiled innocently at him.

"Can I hide under the blanket with you?" Mary's face was dead serious, leaving the adults around her chuckling.

"Yes, I want you snuggled up right beside me. We'll hide under the blanket and pretend we're somewhere else far, far away from here."

Everyone helped to get things packed securely into the wagon. Since the water wasn't too deep along here, or at least according to the men who didn't seem as concerned, they would just lead the teams across. Men on the other side would use ropes as pulleys to steady the wagons from drifting away in the current while they animals pulled it across to the other side.

It sounded so simple when they explained it, but right now, all Jenna was wishing for was a nice solid bridge for them to easily ride across. She thought this was something they should have really tried to perfect with this many travelers making their way along here, but who was she to question history?

She'd studied enough about the Oregon Trail to know that some of the crossings would kill people. Ferries had to be used, or the wagons emptied, caulked, then floated across. And she knew that some of the items they had packed probably wouldn't make it all the way to Oregon.

There were a few things she knew were treasured by Minnie, so she prayed at least those items would make it safely.

Today, though, she needed to focus on just getting to the other side of this river. And, she had to act calm and not at all bothered, so Mary wouldn't sense her worry.

Looking over at Adam, her eyes slammed into his as he stood quietly watching her. He offered her a caring smile, and she knew he was worried too. Knowing him, he would be heavily carrying the weight of getting everyone across safely.

So, she put on her bravest face and smiled back, like she didn't have a worry in the world. The last thing she was going to do was give him anything else to stress about.

As it was, Charlotte had been a wreck all morning, crying and desperately trying to make sure all her belongings were watertight. He didn't need another woman to try soothing.

As the first wagons started to make their way across, with the men all pitching in and helping, she left Mary asking Minnie questions and walked over to Annie. She leaned against the wagon and reached out to scratch the animal under the neck, smiling as the cow lifted her chin and closed her eyes, completely enthralled by the affection.

"Oh, Annie, do you even know how to swim? Do you think Adam would notice if I tried to sneak you into my wagon with me?"

She heard something break and then a man yelling as they made their way through the water, but she couldn't make herself look. Adam was on a horse, helping to steady the wagons from behind, and Jenna knew it was dangerous.

Instead, she was going to keep her head tucked in beside Annie and pretend nothing was happening anywhere else. If she kept talking loud enough, maybe she wouldn't hear the noises on the other side of her wagon.

She continued to stroke the gentle animal while she prayed, until finally, Adam rode up and dismounted beside her. He was soaked from the waist down and she could hear his boots squeaking as he walked over.

"Are you ready?"

She nodded, afraid to say anything in case he sensed her fear.

"I'm going to get you all into the wagons, and then we'll bring them both across together. All the men are helping so everything will be safe. There's nothing to worry about."

"I know. But what about the animals?" She gave Annie one more pat as Minnie and Mary came over.

"Well, Annie is likely a stronger swimmer than any of us here, so she'll be fine. We'll put the chicken crate into the wagon. And the oxen will be able to swim well enough, being pulled through."

"All right, Mary, let's get inside the wagon with that blanket while Mr. Wallace goes to get the other wagon ready." Jenna knew Adam would want to go and offer reassurance to Charlotte too, so she didn't want to hold him up too long here.

Jenna climbed up, then put her arms out to take Mary from Hunter, who was hugging his daughter reassuringly. "Just stay in the wagon with Miss Hart and Mrs. Wallace. They will look after you. I'll see you on the other side."

All the times Jenna had heard about the hardships on these trails, and the deaths, she'd never really put herself in the place of these pioneers who were literally facing it every day. It was so real seeing this man hug his daughter, knowing he had no guarantee they'd both make it across this river.

Anything could go wrong, at any time, and it was a fact of life out here.

It was something the history books had never managed to show—the harsh reality of what happened to so many of these families.

As the wagon slowly started creaking along, Jenna tried to smile bravely at Minnie. The older woman reached over and patted her on the leg.

"All right, Mary. I have our blanket here for us. Let's get underneath and tell each other stories. We'll be across before we know it."

She could tell the moment they were fully in the water as the wagon slowed and felt as though it was floating in air for a moment. Water slapped against the side of the wood, and the world around them was filled with the shouts of the men working to bring them across. She knew one of those men would be doing everything in his power to keep them safe, and it helped to ease her nerves.

Mary was telling her a story about one time when she was riding on a horse and how she was scared, but she didn't fall off. Jenna tried hard to pay attention, but every time the wagon lurched or slipped, her heart stopped. It was hard to remain seated without falling over top of the little girl, but she held her close, hoping she was offering her some comfort.

After what seemed like an eternity, Jenna thought maybe they weren't jostling around as much, so she peeked out of the blanket, hoping to see they would soon be going up the other side of the embankment.

She almost cried out with joy when she realized how close they were. "We're almost there, Mary! See, it wasn't bad at all." Her eyes met Minnie's, who smiled at her knowingly.

The men heaved on the ropes while the oxen strained to take them up the bank. They were almost completely out of the water when a loud cry from an animal in distress reached her ears. She immediately knew it was Annie.

She sat up near the opening, leaning out to try and find her. Her eyes scanned the river behind them, hoping to see her, and praying Adam would be nearby.

As the wagon gave a final lurch out of the water, she could see the cow being pulled by the current, away from the riders in the water who were too busy focusing on the wagons.

"Annie!"

Before she had a chance to think, she jumped over the back, her boots splashing into the water below. It was quite shallow here since they were almost onto the bank, but as she struggled to get out into the water, she realized it was getting deep fast.

She pushed forward, wishing she could take this ridiculous skirt off that was weighing her down. It was making it impossible to move.

Annie mooed loudly, struggling to keep her head above the water. Jenna didn't care what happened—she was not going to stand here and watch the poor animal get dragged away to drown.

"Jenna, what are you doing?" Adam's loud voice boomed across the water, and she could tell he was angry. She looked over just as she saw him let go of the rope holding the back of the wagon and turn the horse to get to her.

"Annie needs help!"

As she shouted the words at him, trying to make him hear over the sounds of the wagons around them, she turned back to see where Annie was now. When she turned, her foot slipped on a rock and she lurched forward, putting her hands out to try and stop herself.

She saw the large rock jutting out of the water just before the pain ripped through her forehead. The last thing she saw as she landed in the water was Adam's furious face as he raced toward her, his mouth opening as he screamed her name.

CHAPTER 13

"Is she awake yet?"

Adam stood up as his mother walked toward him, but she shook her head and put her hand out to tell him to stay sitting.

"No, she's still unconscious. She's got quite the gash on her head, so I'm certain it's going to be excruciating when she wakes up."

They were all sitting around the fire where they'd set up a temporary camp when he'd pulled the wagons ahead. After Jenna had fallen against the rock in the water, he'd managed to grab her before she was dragged away with the current. His mother had hopped out of the wagon and made a bed out of blankets to lie her on, tending to her head.

"Well, why was she getting out of the wagon

before it was stopped anyway? For goodness sakes, you'd think she'd know better." Charlotte shook her head and pretended she was actually concerned about Jenna.

Nelson stood up and limped over to where Jenna was lying on the ground, crouching down until he was sitting next to her. Adam clenched his jaw tight as he fought the anger he felt seeing him there.

"Nelson was terribly distraught when he heard she'd been hurt. I think he's quite taken with her." Charlotte watched her brother as he reached out to push hair back from Jenna's forehead to get a better look at the bump.

Adam silently fumed, hoping Nelson wasn't the one she saw when she opened her eyes. It should be him. He's the one who actually cared about her, even if it wasn't right. Nelson only cared when it suited him.

And if Nelson offered a little bit more help around here, maybe this wouldn't have happened. There would have been an extra set of eyes who could have noticed her coming out of the wagon before it was too late. Instead, he was lounging in the back of a wagon, letting the rest of the men pull him across.

Adam knew he wasn't being fair, but he was

angry. Seeing Jenna fall against the rock had driven the breath from his body. It had seemed to take forever before he was able to grab her and get her out of the water.

When he'd seen the blood pouring from her head, he'd believed he was too late to save her. He hadn't felt a grief that deep since his brother had died.

"She'll be fine. Jenna is made of tough stuff. I'm sure she'll be insisting to still lead the wagon tomorrow."

"Well, she can insist all she wants. She won't be doing it." His voice was angry, making his mother raise an eyebrow in his direction. Charlotte handed him a plate filled with bacon and beans, smiling sweetly while she moved to sit beside him. There was a time when he'd have been over the moon excited that she was so attentive to him.

But right now, Adam just couldn't think about anything except the woman lying unconscious with Nelson hovering over her. Thankfully, his mother must have realized how close he was to taking the other man and throwing him into the river, so she called out for him to come grab some supper.

Nelson hobbled back over, shaking his head

sadly. "I just can't imagine what she was thinking. Over a stupid cow."

Adam glared at Nelson. "It might just be a stupid cow to you, but in case you hadn't noticed, Jenna is the type of person who would care just as much for an animal as a human. I should have known she'd do something like this. I saw Annie starting to struggle but was going to go back to help her when the wagons were secure." He thrust his hand through his hair in frustration. "I should have known she would go in to help her."

"No, she should have listened to what you said and stayed in the wagon. It isn't a woman's place to go jumping into a river to save a silly animal." Charlotte wasn't looking too happy with him, obviously not appreciating the concern he was showing for the other woman.

They finished eating in silence, all of them lost in their own thoughts until he noticed Jenna starting to move out of the corner of his eye. His fury at the situation swept through him again, and he quickly stood up, storming over to her. He had full intentions of giving her a piece of his mind for what she'd done.

But when he looked down and saw the bruise on her head, as she reached up to tenderly touch it, his anger rushed out of his body. And when she looked up at him with those blue eyes, he knew he couldn't be mad at her. He was just so glad she was all right.

He crouched down next to her while the others came up behind him. "Don't try moving too much. You've taken a pretty hard knock on the head, so it's best to just stay lying down."

He wanted to lift her into his arms again and take her away from everyone else, so he could tell her how scared he'd been. But he knew it wasn't something he could ever do.

"Where's Annie?" Her voice sounded scared as she finally remembered everything.

He closed his eyes in frustration and sighed loudly before looking at her again. "Annie is fine. As she would have been if you'd just left her. Did I not tell you she could swim?"

"Yes, but she was struggling. I couldn't just leave her."

"You could have left her, Jenna. Within seconds of you cracking your head on the rock, she was able to swim herself out of the current and up onto the other side. Now, she's happily grazing on the other side of the wagon, completely unaware of the trouble she caused."

Jenna's face fell slightly, and she looked down.

"I'm sorry that I caused extra trouble for everyone. I figured the water wasn't deep so it would be easy to go in."

Adam wanted to shake her and hug her at the same time. "And, I'm curious what you thought you were going to do once you did get to her?"

She lifted her eyes to his and shrugged. "I hadn't really thought it all out very well."

"Would you like something to eat, dear?" Minnie had crouched down next to him and pushed her hair back to look at the gash. "We should try cleaning this up a bit more too."

"I'm fine. I can sit up to have lunch." Suddenly, her mouth opened, and she looked around in shock. "It is lunchtime, isn't it? I mean, how long was I out?"

Relief flooded through Adam as he realized she was fine. She was back to speaking in a way he'd never heard anyone else talk.

"It's actually an early supper. You were 'out' for a few hours, and none of us really felt like eating lunch by the time we got everything else sorted out."

She looked around at all of them. "I'm sorry. I made a mess of everything today."

His mother reached out and took her hand. "Don't you say that. We're all just glad you're all right. Now, let's get some hot food into you."

Adam leaned in and let her put his arm around his shoulder to bring her to a sitting position. Nelson scowled at him, but Adam didn't care. The man had been hobbling around for days, barely offering to carry anything, so how did he expect to help Jenna sit upright?

Just then, Mary came running over with Hunter not far behind. "Miss Hart, you're okay!"

The little girl ran into her shoulders and wrapped her arms around them, almost knocking her over. Thankfully, he had a good hold on her and was able to keep her upright.

"Mary, I told you to be careful. Miss Hart is likely feeling a bit sore right now." Her father chastised his daughter as he came over and looked at Jenna. "It's good to see you sitting up. When I saw Adam scooping you out of the water, I admit I thought the worst."

"I thought you'd *died*, Miss Hart!"

Mary started to cry, the worry and upset from the day catching up to her. Jenna put her free arm around the little girl and held her tightly against her.

"Oh, Mary, I'm sorry for scaring you like that. But I didn't die. I'm perfectly fine. Well, except for this big goose-egg on my head."

Mary giggled, bringing her hand up to her mouth. "You have a goose egg on your head?"

He watched as Jenna looked at him with what almost looked like panic in her eyes as she tried to explain her strange way of explaining the bump. He'd never heard anyone call it that before, so he figured it must be a New York expression.

"Not a real egg. It just looks like one because it's such a big bump. I think I'd like to stand up, please."

He helped her up and walked her over to a more comfortable spot, with Mary stuck to her one side, and him trying to hold her upright on the other. She tucked in perfectly beneath his arm as he kept her close, not wanting to let her fall.

As he eased her down, she stumbled slightly but quickly recovered, glancing around, perhaps hoping no one else had seen. "This looks delicious, Charlotte."

She offered a smile to the other woman who turned away and walked to her wagon without a word. Jenna glanced at him guiltily, and he suspected Jenna knew Charlotte was jealous at the attention he was giving to her.

Adam knew he'd likely given himself away today as far as his feelings toward Jenna, and now he felt even more trapped. How was he going to get out of this mess?

Would he have to marry Charlotte out of loyalty and obligation? Or was there any way he could possibly follow his heart?

Even as he let himself be excited for a brief moment, he knew deep down the kind of man he was. He was honor bound to marry the woman who had followed him all this way.

And it didn't matter what his heart had to say about it.

CHAPTER 14

*J*enna walked slowly to where the small fire still crackled. Minnie and Charlotte were sleeping by now, having turned in early after their trying day, but her own head was aching too much to get any sleep. In fact, her whole body ached but she would never admit it to anyone. She'd waited until she saw Nelson leave for his nightly game of cards, before crawling out of the tent. Adam had said he was going to speak with Luke about their upcoming stop at Fort Kearny, so she'd have some time alone to sit and think.

She wasn't sure if it was from the knock on the head, or just the accumulation of everything from the days on the trail, but today she was ready to give up. Maybe she'd made a mistake by coming here.

Seeing Adam every day, and knowing he wasn't the man she was supposed to find and fall in love with, was killing her. She couldn't believe how easily it had happened, but it had. And, she was finally willing to admit it to her heart.

No matter how hard she'd tried to find something with Nelson, like she was feeling for Adam, it just wouldn't happen. Her eyes would be drawn back to the one who made her heart race every time he even looked at her.

And now, she had a feeling he might be starting to feel something for her too. She knew it was silly, especially since the woman he was going to marry was beautiful and perfect in every way, but Jenna sensed something whenever he was around her.

She'd seen it today when he'd helped her after she'd woken up, and she was pretty sure Charlotte had too.

Jenna never wanted to be that other woman who caused problems. She knew what it was like to be the one getting hurt by it, and she couldn't do that to another woman. Even someone like Charlotte.

So, now what was she supposed to do? Stay here with weeks of close contact left with the man she was in love with? Seeing him every single day, and knowing when they made it to Oregon, he would marry Charlotte.

Because one thing she'd learned about Adam already was that he was an honorable man who took his word seriously. Even though he might never have actually offered marriage to Charlotte, the fact that it had always been assumed and she followed him west, meant he was left with no other choice in his mind.

"You should be sleeping. After the knock you took today, you need to rest."

His voice startled her as he walked toward her. She'd been so lost in her thoughts she hadn't even heard him coming. When she lifted her eyes and met his, her heart ached with the emotion she was feeling.

He came over and sat on a crate next to her by the fire, his eyes never leaving hers. "How's your head feeling?"

She shrugged and looked into the fire. "It's sore. But I don't think it's hurt as badly as my pride." She sheepishly lifted her gaze back up to his. "I know what I did was stupid, but when I saw Annie being pulled away in the river, I just panicked. I'm used to handling things myself, so I reacted before thinking."

He stared at her for what seemed like forever,

before finally speaking again. "I'm sorry that you've had to handle things by yourself. But now you've got other people who can help you, if you let them."

She tried to laugh to break up the seriousness of the moment. "Well, I know, but I'd much prefer to do things like jumping out of a wagon into a raging river to save a cow. Who didn't even need saving in the first place."

He smiled and nodded, finally looking away. She let out the breath she'd been holding. But he was still sitting too close and she could feel the heat from his body. The fire crackled, mixing with the sounds of the animals around the wagons who were settling in for the night. She wished this moment would never end—just the two of them with no one else around.

"When I saw you fall into the water, I have to admit I was scared. I mean, if anything had happened to you, I couldn't have lived with myself."

She watched his profile as the flickering of the flames moved the shadows over his face. "Adam, if anything had happened to me, it would have been my own fault. Not yours. You can't always take every responsibility onto your own shoulders."

He shrugged and leaned forward to rest his arms on his legs, staring at the ground. "It wasn't just worry from the responsibility of you being in my care that scared me. I was afraid of losing you."

He spoke so low, she almost didn't hear him. He lifted his gaze and she could feel the raw emotion in them. Before she knew what was happening, he'd turned slightly, reaching out to tenderly push her hair from her forehead. Everywhere his fingers touched her skin left a trail of heat. She swallowed, trying to calm her racing heart.

His hand moved along her hairline and his eyes followed everywhere his fingers went. When his hand gently moved behind her head to pull her closer, she was already moving toward him.

His head lowered and his lips covered hers, slowly moving over them while his hand caressed her neck. His other arm wrapped around her, holding her close and steadying her on the crate. She was completely leaning into him, and she brought her hands up to his chest where the pounding of his heart could be felt through his shirt.

Just when she was sure she couldn't remember how to breathe, he lifted his head and stared down into her eyes. She could see the sadness in his.

"I'm sorry, I shouldn't have done that."

When he pulled away, she almost cried out in pain. Being in his arms had felt right, and now the cold of the evening seeped in, leaving her feeling more alone than ever.

But he stayed sitting right next to her as he stared into the fire, the tension between them palpable. She knew the confusion in his mind, because she was trying to figure it all out too.

He quickly turned to look at her, catching her off guard. "So…what are your plans when you get out west? I worry that you'll just be on your own."

As awkward as this was, she welcomed the distraction. But how could she tell him her plans, when she had no idea herself? She'd been a waitress back home, so that was probably her only skill. But she wasn't sure how many jobs were available to single women in this time.

"I'll be fine. I'm going to get a job and will just start my new life." Her heart was breaking as she imagined that new life without Adam in it. After their kiss, she didn't even want to think about it. Surely there had to be a way.

She was sure no one else was awake in the world as they sat, the crackling of the fire, and the lowing of the animals the only noise around them. The silence out here at night was almost deafening at times.

"Can I ask… I know this is a little forward of me, but…"

Jenna almost laughed. And kissing her hadn't been?

"What did he do to you? Why did you have to leave? I know it's none of my concern, but what if he does find you?"

She was shocked as he brought up the subject of her ex. Guilt ate at her, knowing he'd probably been worrying about this man she'd mentioned who had hurt her and wanted to find her.

"He won't find me here."

Adam's eyes locked on hers. "How do you know for sure?" The worry he held for her was genuine and it was like something he couldn't let go of.

As she held his gaze, she knew he was someone she could trust. Someone she could count on. Even if he wasn't someone she could love. And she realized with a sinking feeling, even though they'd shared a kiss and he obviously had feelings for her, there was never any chance for them.

It was time to just tell him the truth and let him decide what he wanted to believe. She needed to just put everything out there. If she couldn't be with him, he at least deserved to know the truth about her. At least he wouldn't worry about her being hurt by her ex if he wasn't going to be around to protect her.

"Adam, you know how you've asked me where I'm from? Well, I'm from New York, that's true. But, I'm from New York, over one hundred and fifty years in the future. That's how I know my ex won't find me here."

He swallowed and shook his head slowly. "Jenna, I think you took a pretty big bump on your head and might be a bit confused, but please, just tell me the truth. I need to know that even if I'm not around to protect you, you will be safe from him."

"I'm telling you the truth, Adam, whether you choose to believe me or not. I came here thanks to a woman who can grant wishes. She was supposed to be a matchmaker, who could find a person's soul mate in another time. I know it's hard to believe, but I promise, it's true. The problem with the magic she performed this time is that it didn't work right. I think it was a mistake for me to come here."

As she said the words, her heart broke at the pain in his eyes. He didn't believe her, and probably all he heard was about it being a mistake. But she also knew she was the one who had to make the hard decision.

Because she knew Adam and he couldn't let

anyone down, he'd be torn between his loyalty and honor, and the guilt of leaving her alone if she was in danger.

And she couldn't do that to him. She would help make his decision easier.

Even if it meant her own heart was broken.

dam stared ahead as the fort came into view. Charlotte was talking excitedly about being able to see a bit of civilization out here after being "stuck with the same people" for days on end.

He wasn't sure what she thought Fort Kearney was going to be like, but he knew she was going to be in for a surprise. It wasn't a bustling town filled with the amenities she was used to.

As it had for the past couple of days, his mind went to Jenna. He hadn't been able to think about anything else after their kiss the other night. He'd known in that moment she was the one he needed to be with. Every time he thought about leaving her at the end of the trail, and possibly in danger, his heart ached.

She had tried to make him believe some nonsense about being from the future, and he wasn't sure why she would tell him that. He knew she was trying to make the danger she was in less worrisome for him, but surely she didn't think he'd actually believe her.

"I'm so glad you asked me to come with you today, Adam. We never get to spend any time alone together. It seems like either your mother, or that woman who joined us uninvited, are always underfoot."

Adam clenched his jaw. He needed to remember he'd known Charlotte for a long time, and he did care for her. She didn't deserve what he was about to do, and it tore him apart.

But he'd made up his mind. He wanted what his mother and father had shared. And he would never have that with Charlotte.

As they pulled into the fort, he stopped the wagon and pulled on the brake. He turned to face Charlotte, hoping she would understand.

"Charlotte, we need to talk about what will happen when we get to Oregon."

She laughed and reached out to tap his knee. "Adam, are you proposing to me?"

He swallowed, wishing he could make this easier. "I told you before we left, I wasn't ready to get married yet. I wanted to go west and have the adventure my uncle Mike never got the chance to have before he died. He always said it was his biggest regret."

She was watching him carefully, seeming to understand this wasn't the proposal she'd been hoping for. Her skin was perfectly flawless, and not showing any signs of having been on the trail all this time. Her hair was tucked under her bonnet with just a few pieces charmingly poking out to frame her beauty.

There was a time he thought she was all he could ever want.

Now, he knew that even before he'd left home, his heart already knew she wasn't. He just hadn't known how to admit it.

"Well, your uncle Mike was a grumpy old bachelor, and I'm not really sure why we're talking about him right now."

"Because I think he was trying to tell me something I hadn't realized for myself. That there was more out there than the little town I lived in. And, I think he knew if I stayed there, I'd end up choosing a life that would never make me happy."

"What would he know? He had more money than sense anyway."

Adam pulled his eyebrows together and laughed softly. "Uncle Mike didn't have any money."

Her mouth opened and she glared at him. "What do you mean? Everyone said your uncle was rich, and he had no heirs except you."

Adam couldn't figure out what she was talking about. He'd heard a few rumors over the years but had always laughed it off, knowing how much his uncle loved to spend his money on his weekly card games.

Suddenly, everything hit him. The sudden interest Charlotte paid to him. Nelson giving up the mercantile back home to come west. He even told Adam one night not that long ago that he would have to pitch in money for Charlotte to have her dress shop area in his new mercantile.

It all made sense now.

"You thought I had inherited money from my uncle. That's why you wanted to come west with me. And your brother thought he could leech off it too and build something bigger out west than he could ever have back home."

"Adam, you're lying to me. You inherited everything from your uncle."

He laughed, shaking his head in disbelief. "You're right, I did inherit everything. And that included his business, which I sold to be able to start up my new blacksmith shop when I get to Oregon. It will barely be enough to do that. Oh, and an old hammer he always used that I thought I'd like to keep as a memento of everything he taught me."

"So, you have no money?"

Charlotte's voice was getting higher with every word she spoke. Her eyes were wide and her already flawlessly white skin was even paler.

"Not the kind you're talking about."

She stared at him for a moment, and he watched as her cheeks reddened with anger.

"I can't believe you lied to me like this. Just to get me to come with you all the way out here."

By now, Adam was fighting the urge to laugh out loud at how ridiculous this whole situation was. All this time, he had been feeling obligated to marry Charlotte because she'd come west, out of the love she had for him.

When all she really had was love for his money. Money that he didn't even have.

He was surprised how calm he was feeling about these revelations. Instead of feeling hurt for being used, and knowing she never really cared about him, he felt free.

She was never meant to be the woman he spent the rest of his life with.

"WHAT DO you mean you can't find her? I would have seen her if she'd walked to the fort. There's wide open space between there and where we're camped out. She has to be here somewhere."

"Adam, I'm telling you, I've looked everywhere. No one has seen her. She seemed disheartened today after you asked Charlotte to ride into the fort with you for supplies." His mother wrung her hands together as she always did when she was worried. "Nelson was laughing excitedly, saying you were likely finally going to marry Charlotte since there'd be someone at Fort Kearney who'd be able to perform the ceremony."

Adam thrust his hand into his hair, almost knocking his hat onto the ground. "Of course, he was excited. He thought he was about to get money for his bigger mercantile out west. I can't believe I ever fell for any of this. All of a sudden Charlotte had so much interest in me, after all the years of never giving me the time of day."

If Nelson was still here, he'd likely strangle him right now. But he'd gone off to the fort with his wagon as soon as Adam had returned to let him know there would never be a marriage between him and his sister, and that she wasn't spending another day on this trail. She'd said she'd stay at Fort Kearney, and they would be turning around at the earliest possible moment.

But now, Jenna was missing, and he was at a loss as to where she could have gone. It wasn't like there were a lot of hiding places out here.

He walked over to the wagon and looked inside again. Where would she have gone? Her trunk was still inside, so she couldn't be far.

"Adam, I feel like she was saying goodbye to me. I don't know how to explain it, but I caught her over here talking to Annie and hugging her, if you can imagine. When I came along, I could see she'd been crying, but I didn't say anything about it." His mother paced in circles as she talked. "Then, she came and hugged me too, telling me how much she appreciated me. And that she'd never had a ma, but if she had, she wished she would have been like me.

She thanked me for not leaving her back in Independence."

His mother started to shake her head slowly as tears welled up in her eyes. "I just don't know why, but in my heart, I feel like she was saying goodbye. But where would she go?"

Hunter came over with Mary right behind him. "Have you found her yet? I've asked around again, but she's nowhere to be found."

Hunter had been helping him look since he got back, and Mary was visibly upset, with tears running down her cheeks.

Adam just shook his head in confusion. He'd asked everyone in the entire wagon train, and no one had seen her. It was like she'd just vanished into thin air.

Suddenly, his stomach lurched. He looked in and saw her trunk sitting there, and he remembered the day he'd met her. He'd stumbled over top of her all of a sudden lying on the ground with that trunk beside her.

Out of nowhere.

Jumping into the back of the wagon, his heart clenched in agony as he started to realize what he was seeing. He threw the trunk open and started throwing the clothes off the top. As soon as he saw the items underneath, he knew.

She hadn't been lying to him. He pulled out bottles he'd never seen before, in a strange material, that were both hard and soft when he squeezed them, reading the words. "Sunscreen? Protection against UV rays? What does that mean?" he muttered to himself. He squeezed some onto the back of his hand and recognized the scent he could always smell on her. It sent another pang of worry into his stomach. The sharp ache of knowing she could be gone forever.

On the very bottom of the trunk, was a small rectangular shaped item he'd never seen before. He lifted it up, suddenly feeling dizzy with the realization of the truth. This wasn't something from this time. It had a cover and when he opened it, it was black and hard, in a strange material again. There were buttons or something on the sides, but no matter how hard he tried, he couldn't imagine what it would be.

He sat back, holding it in his hands as he realized she was gone. And where she'd gone, he had no way to get her back.

"Oh, Adam. Where is she?"

His mother sounded just as heartbroken and he

realized how much Jenna had come to mean to all of them in the short time they'd known her.

Just when he was sure his world was crumbling around him, he noticed something tucked into a pocket in the cover of the strange object he was holding. Pulling it out, he read it out loud, *"Dr. Lachele Simpson—Matchrimony, Matchmaker Extraordinaire."*

He remembered Jenna saying something about a woman who granted wishes and was supposed to help her find her soul mate in another time. She said there had been a mistake and she shouldn't have been here.

Adam knew, without a doubt, she was exactly where she was supposed to be. But now, it was too late, and he'd never be able to tell her.

He vaguely heard Hunter tell his mother they should give him some time alone. His mother still didn't know what was going on, but Hunter had obviously seen enough to understand it was significant.

Adam sat there in the wagon wishing he could have said goodbye. Wishing he could have just had the chance to tell her he loved her.

"Oh, my goodness. This is even dustier and smaller than I'd ever imagined."

Adam jumped as someone spoke from the far side of the wagon. His head whipped around to see a woman with purple hair sitting on top of a chest his mother had insisted on bringing. This woman was wearing a colorful type of gown that almost matched her hair perfectly, and she'd shown up out of nowhere.

He opened his mouth but didn't even know what to say.

She clapped her hands together and looked at him expectantly. "Well, I'm a very busy woman. I can grant wishes, but I'm not going to sit here all day. There's a young lady I believe is wishing just as hard to see you right now, but the difference is, she's trying to pretend she isn't."

"Dr. Lachelle?" he asked in disbelief.

"That would be me," she announced heartily.

Adam sat in shock for a second. This was his chance. If this crazy-looking woman was able to grant his wish, he had to try.

He needed to see Jenna one more time.

He hopped out of the wagon and ran over to where his mother was standing with Hunter. "Can you look after my mother for me? If I go away for a while?"

"What are you talking about, Adam?" His mother

was looking at him like he'd lost his mind, and he realized maybe he had.

"Ma, I love you. I hope you know that. But I have the chance to go find Jenna, and I don't know what will happen." He looked at Hunter. "If I don't get back, can you make sure she gets to Oregon?"

"Adam, what are you doing?"

"I'm going to find the woman I love and beg her to come back with me. But, if she won't, I will have no other choice but to stay there with her."

CHAPTER 16

Jenna sat in the window seat that looked out to the busy street. She had her legs pulled up tightly to her chest with her chin resting on her knees and a blanket wrapped around herself. This was how she'd been for the past few hours since she'd come back. She didn't know how the time difference worked, so she didn't know how long it had been since Adam had found out she was gone.

Or if he'd even cared.

Seeing him drive off with Charlotte had helped her make her decision. She'd already known she had to leave, to let Adam live the life he was supposed to live. It wasn't her place to mess with history when he was meant to be with someone else.

She jumped as her phone vibrated on the table. Carly had kept it for her, perhaps hoping her friend would come back and need it someday. Her eyes met Carly's as her friend walked into the room. "He just doesn't give up, does he?"

When she'd been "poofed" back, she'd come to Carly's knowing her apartment would be gone. She'd given up the lease and sold everything she had before she left, never thinking she'd be back here.

While she'd been so happy to see her friends, everything now just seemed so wrong. When she'd first gone back in time to that wagon train headed west, she hadn't felt like she belonged there. And it took her some time, but she'd started to feel like it was right to be there.

She hadn't wanted to ask Dr. Lachele if she was the only one of her matches who had failed because she didn't want to know the answer. It was hard enough knowing she'd let herself fall in love with the wrong person she'd been sent back for, without also being the one person who'd messed up their chance.

When she'd said goodbye to Minnie, it had hurt so badly. She'd finally started to believe she had someone who would be like a mother figure to her, something she'd never had before. She loved Minnie with her whole heart and having to leave her too had been devastating.

She even missed Annie something fierce. She leaned her head against the cool window pane and closed her eyes, letting herself remember the sweet animal she'd bonded with. No one would have ever believed Jenna Hart would end up so attached to a silly cow.

Suddenly, a loud commotion at the back door made Jenna whip her head around to meet Carly's scared gaze.

"Do you think he knows you're here?" her friend whispered as she slowly made her way to peek out the window by the door. She pulled the curtain back and looked outside, then turned and looked at Jenna with wide eyes.

Jenna's heart stopped. Had Dave shown up for her?

"It's Dr. Lachele." She quickly went and opened the door for the woman who had just left Jenna here this morning.

"I haven't been back and forth this much since that time I rode on that swing ride at the fair that left me feeling quite sick. The things I do for love!"

Dr. Lachele never just said hello when she entered a room. She entered a room and let her presence be known with flair. But it was the man walking in behind her that had Jenna's heart in her throat.

"Carly, dear, I'm in need of something to drink. All this poofing back and forth is quite exhausting. Would you make me a cup of tea while we let these two figure out that Dr. Lachele never makes a mistake when it comes to matters of the heart."

When they were alone, Adam slowly started to walk toward her. She was still wrapped in her blanket, and in her haste to get up, her foot tangled in the frayed edge, and she started to fall.

He caught her before she hit the floor and pulled her upright, helping her to untangle from the blanket. When she lifted her eyes to his, her chest clenched with emotion.

"Why are you here?" Her voice cracked as she tried to speak over the lump in her throat. His hands were still holding her steady as the blanket finally fell to the floor.

He smiled, then reached one hand up to gently touch her cheek. "Jenna, did you honestly think I was going to let you leave like that? Without even giving me a chance to tell you I love you, and I don't ever want to imagine my life without you."

"But...how...?"

Had he just said he loved her?

"Well, when I got back after taking Charlotte to tell her I couldn't marry her, I discovered the woman I wanted to see, and tell how happy I was to have in my life, had vanished. Luckily, I am not the type of man to give up easily and the next thing I knew, there was a purple-haired woman sitting beside me, telling me I had one chance to find you."

Jenna was trying to listen to everything, but as he spoke, he was moving his fingers along her jaw, looking at her with his heart in his gaze.

"You weren't going to marry Charlotte? But, if she was the one you were supposed to marry, we can't change history."

"No, I wasn't going to marry her. I'd decided that after I kissed you. I knew then my heart belonged to you."

"But, don't you see? That wasn't supposed to happen. You would have married her if I hadn't gone there."

He shook his head. "No, I wouldn't have. It took me a while to figure it out, but I know she was never meant for me. Trust me, one more week on the trail with her, and I'm sure I'd have offered to take her back home myself."

She desperately wanted to believe everything he was saying. But what if…

"Jenna, you were sent to me. I don't understand what is happening, and all of this is so unbelievable, but I know what I feel when I'm with you. You can't ever say you coming to me was a mistake. It's the only thing in my life I can say without a doubt was meant to be."

His head lowered to hers, and when his lips found hers, she knew it was true. This was right. Being in his arms was where she belonged.

Another loud bang on the back door broke them apart. This time, she could hear Dave yelling from the other side. "I know you're in there, Jenna."

Adam's eyes filled with anger, but she just held his arm and shook her head as Dr. Lachele and Carly walked into the room.

"So, are you staying here to deal with a lunatic who won't take no for an answer? Or, will you go back to where I sent you in the first place, and this time believe I did it right?"

"I want to talk to that man." Adam's jaw looked like it was clenching as he fought against the anger she could feel in his arm as she held it tightly.

"No, Adam. Let's just go." She looked at Carly

apologetically. "I'm sorry to leave you to get rid of him. Will you be okay?"

Dr. Lachele waved her hand dramatically. "She'll have me here. And no man can stand up to Dr. Lachele. Now, make your wish."

Jenna looked up into Adam's eyes and wished with her heart. "I wish I could go back to the life I had on the Oregon Trail; with the man I love."

When she opened her eyes again, she was wrapped in his arms, alone in the back of the packed wagon. He was smiling down at her.

"Did you mean it?"

She couldn't understand what he was asking. Her mind was still a bit fuzzy from everything and she was lying sideways on top of something digging into her hip. She shifted to try standing up, so they could get out of the cramped space.

But he held her hand firmly, not letting her move.

"Did you mean it? You're stuck here with me now, so I need to know this is truly what your heart wants."

She stared into his eyes and finally understood what he was asking. She leaned into him and rested her head on his chest, smiling with pure happiness as his arms folded around her.

"Yes, Adam, I love you. I love you with all of my heart, and I know without a doubt, this is where I'm meant to be."

When he reached down and lifted her chin to look back up at him before lowering his lips to hers, she knew she was where she had always belonged.

Jenna leaned down to scratch Annie's neck, smiling as the animal lifted her head in the air. "I can't believe how much has happened since the day we met. We've already been through so much, and we have many more weeks on this trail, but I know we're tough. We're going to make it to Oregon. Just, promise me no more water scares, okay? Maybe next time I will insist that you come in the wagon with me."

She laughed softly, shaking her head at herself. Here she stood, nowhere near civilization, over a century before she had even been born, talking to a cow on her wedding day.

It was like something from a really bizarre movie

written by someone who had a seriously twisted mind.

"Miss Hart, it's so beautiful today. This is the perfect day for you and Mr. Wallace to get married. I can't wait to be your flower girl."

Mary came running over, quickly giving her a hug before turning her attention to Annie. "We should find a ribbon to dress Annie up too!"

Jenna laughed and shook her head. "I don't think Mr. Wallace would be very happy if we brought Annie to the wedding. She can stay here and enjoy the nice grass while we all have fun."

Minnie came around the back of the wagon and laughed when she saw her and Mary standing there. "Why did I know you two would be back here keeping company with Annie?" She came over and patted Mary on the head. "You run along and get your fancy dress on for the wedding. Your pa is looking for you."

"All right, Mrs. Wallace." Mary grinned at Jenna. "I can't wait!" She quickly turned and ran back to her own wagon to get ready. The poor child had been a bundle of excitement ever since they'd told her they were getting married.

After they'd come back, Adam had told her he didn't want to wait to get married. There was a reverend traveling with them, and he figured there was no point in waiting any longer. He hadn't come right out and said it, but he'd implied that with the dangers ahead, he wanted to know she always had the protection of his name if anything were to happen.

For miles, they'd seen the giant rock formation that seemed to reach into the sky as they moved toward it. Luke had said when they made it to the rock, they would stop for the day to rest. After this point, the terrain would get a bit rougher as they moved out of the prairies, so he wanted everyone to have the chance to rest.

And, since they were making good time, he figured it might be a good day to celebrate a wedding.

Minnie walked right up to her and took her hands in hers, smiling at her warmly. "Jenna, I can't tell you how happy I am that you're becoming my daughter today. You're exactly the kind of girl I'd always hoped my son would find to love him." She gently squeezed her hands. "And, you're exactly the daughter I'd hoped for myself."

Tears welled up in Jenna's eyes as she looked at this woman who'd become the closest thing she'd ever had to a mom. "Thank you, Minnie. I know I've said it before but thank you from the bottom of my heart for not leaving me behind in Independence. You could have walked away and not taken on the burden of having me along, but you didn't."

Minnie chuckled softly. "I sensed something in you that day, and I knew in my heart, you were somehow meant to be in my life. So, today after you marry my son, I hope you will consider calling me Ma."

Jenna reached out to hug her, the tears now flowing freely down her cheeks. "You'll never know how long I've wanted to have someone to be my mom."

They stood hugging for a while, neither wanting the moment to end. Finally, the sound of a man clearing his throat interrupted them. "I'm sorry to intrude, but I was hoping maybe I could have a moment alone with my bride before we go ahead and say our vows."

Minnie pulled away, wiping at her eyes. "Of course. I need to go change into something a little less dusty anyway."

They watched the older woman walk away, then Adam turned and came to stand right in front of her. Annie stuck her nose out toward him, trying to push him away. She laughed at the frown he directed at the cow. "She's just hoping I will get back to scratching her neck, and you're in my way."

He stood his ground and shook his head. "I'm not moving, Annie, so you may as well go back to eating." When he finally lifted his head and met her eyes, Jenna's breath caught.

The love she could see reflected back at her was something she'd never tire of seeing. It was something she'd only dreamed about, and had thought was only true in romance novels.

Yet, here she was standing face to face with someone who she knew beyond a doubt was the man she would spend the rest of her days with. And she had never looked more forward to anything in her life.

He'd shaved this morning, saying he wanted to look his best, but already a dark shadow was starting to show on his face. Her hand reached up to rest against his cheek, feeling the scratchy surface as he leaned his head into her hand.

He brought his hand up to hold hers, then placed a gentle kiss on the back of it.

"Jenna, I know you've agreed to marry me, and you have no idea how happy that makes me. You know I love you with all my heart. But I need to make sure you're ready for the commitment we're about to make. I don't want you to have any regrets."

Jenna's brows pulled together in confusion. "How could you think I'd have any regrets?"

His throat moved as he swallowed, and he reached out to take her other hand in his. "Well, I saw where you came from. The fancy house with so many comfortable things you just won't have here. Everything is going to be different, and it's not going to be easy for you. I wish I could give you what you had back home, but it's just not something I can offer."

He pulled her toward him, and she could feel the heat from his body as they looked into each other's eyes.

"If it meant it would make you happy, and I would never lose you, I'd be willing to go back with you to your time to live. I want you to be where you'll be happy."

For the second time in just a few short minutes, tears started welling up in her eyes again. At this rate, she was going to end up dehydrated by nightfall.

"Adam, don't you understand that I am exactly where I'm supposed to be? I love you, and this is where my heart belongs. This is the life I want to live."

She could understand his worry, but she knew she would never want to go back to the life she'd been living. Sure, there may have been more amenities than what she'd have out here, but already she could see how much more people meant to each other, compared to things, and this was how she wanted to live.

As long as Adam was with her, she knew she could never live anywhere else.

He reached a hand up, gently rubbing his thumb along her jaw. "Are you sure?"

"I've never been more sure of anything. This was where I was always meant to be. This is where I'm happy. I have a ma now, who I love and who I know will love me. And we get to share this beautiful day with all these people who have become a part of our life." She swallowed against the lump in her throat, wanting to get the words out before she couldn't speak. "But most of all, I have a man I love more than anything else in the world. This is where I have always wanted to be."

His head lowered to hers, but before their lips met, Annie's nose pushed in between them, and she mooed loudly. Adam groaned softly, trying to push her nose away.

Jenna laughed and reached out to pat the fuzzy head. "Oh, I'm so sorry, Annie. Of course, how could I forget you?" She grinned up at Adam who rolled his eyes, still holding her close to him as he struggled to keep Annie from getting between them.

This time, as he lowered his head, his lips found hers. And she knew in her heart she wouldn't trade the life she'd been given for all the luxuries in the world back home.

Because in his arms, she finally knew what it meant to be loved.

I HOPE YOU ENJOYED READING, Jenna's Journey. If you could take a couple minutes and head back to the retailer you purchased from to leave a review, it would be greatly appreciated :)

The next book in the series features all of the characters you've already fallen in love with as we continue along the Oregon Trail in Carly's story!

CARLY'S COURAGE - BOOK 2 - IS AVAILABLE ON ALL MAJOR PLATFORMS

ABOUT THE AUTHOR

USA Today Bestselling Author, Kay P. Dawson writes sweet western romance - the kind that leaves out all of the juicy details and immerses you in a true, heartfelt love story. Growing up pretending she was Laura Ingalls, she's always had a love for the old west and pioneer times. She believes in true love, and finding your happy ever after.

Happily married mom of two girls, Kay has always taught her children to follow their dreams. And, after a breast cancer diagnosis at the age of 39, she realized it was time to take her own advice. She had always wanted to write a book, and she decided that the someday she was waiting for was now.

She writes western historical, contemporary and time travel romance that all transport the reader to a time or place where true love always finds a way.

You can connect with Kay through her website at **KayPDawson.com**

**She also has an active fan group where she

hangs out with her readers...**https://www.facebook.com/groups/kaypdawsonfans/**

****Newsletter SignUp:**

https://www.kaypdawson.com/newsletter

****Bookbub Follow:**

https://www.bookbub.com/authors/kay-p-dawson

kaypdawsonwrites@gmail.com

Copyright © 2020 by Kay P. Dawson

All rights reserved.

No part of this book may be reproduced in any form or by any electronic or mechanical means, including information storage and retrieval systems, without written permission from the author, except for the use of brief quotations in a book review.

This book is a work of fiction. Any similarities to people, living or dead, is purely coincidental.

Cover Design - EDH Graphics

Edited - Meg Amor